1

The Story of Hiawatha, Adapted from Longfellow

by Henry Wadsworth Longfellow and Winston Stokes

Copyright © 10/22/2015
Jefferson Publication

ISBN-13: 978-1518737404

Printed in the United States of America

Table of Contents

I

THE PEACE-PIPE

LONG ago, when our cities were pleasant woodlands and the white man was far beyond the seas, the great Manito, God of all the Indians, descended to the earth. From the red crags of the Great Red Pipestone Quarry he gazed upon the country that he ruled, and a silver river gushed from his footprints and turned to gold as it met the morning sun. The Great Manito stooped to gather some of the red stone of the quarry, and molded it with giant fingers into a mighty pipe-bowl; he plucked a reed from the river bank for a pipe-stem, filled the pipe with the bark of the willow, breathed upon the forest until the great boughs chafed together into flame, and there alone upon the mountains he smoked the pipe of peace. The smoke rose high and slowly in the air. Far above the tops of the tallest pine-trees it rose in a thin blue line, so that all the nations might see and hasten at the summons of the Great Manito; and the smoke as it rose grew thicker and purer and whiter, rolling and unfolding in the air until it glistened like a great white fleecy cloud that touched the top of heaven. The Indians saw it from the Valley of Wyoming, and from Tuscaloosa and the far-off Rocky Mountains, and their prophets said: "Come and obey the summons of the Great Manito, who calls the tribes of men to council!"

Over the prairies, down the rivers, through the forests, from north and south and east and west, the red men hastened to approach the smoke-cloud. There were Delawares and Dacotahs and Choctaws and Comanches and Pawnees and Blackfeet and Shoshonies,—all the tribes of Indians in the world, and one and all they gathered at the Pipestone Quarry, where the Great Manito stood and waited for them. And the Great Manito saw that they glared at one another angrily, and he stretched his right hand over them and said:

"My children, I have given you a happy land, where you may fish and hunt. I have filled the rivers with the trout and sturgeon. There are wild fowl in the lakes and marshes; there are bears in the forest and bison on the prairie. Now listen to my warning, for I am weary of your endless quarrels: I will send a Prophet to you, who shall guide you and teach you and share your sufferings. Obey him, and all will be well with you. Disobey him, and you shall be scattered like the autumn leaves. Wash the war-paint and the bloodstains from your bodies; mould the red stone of the quarry into peace-pipes, and smoke with me the pipe of peace and brotherhood that shall last forever."

The tones of his deep voice died away, and the Indians broke their weapons and bathed in the sparkling river. They took the red stone of the quarry and made peace-pipes and gathered in a circle; and while they smoked the Great Manito grew taller and mightier and lighter until he drifted on the smoke high above the clouds into the heavens.

II

THE FOUR WINDS

IN the far-off kingdom of Wabasso, the country of the North-wind, where the fierce blasts howl among the gorges and the mountains are like flint the year round, Mishe Mokwa, the huge bear, had his cave. Years had passed since the great Manito had spoken to the tribes of men, and his words of warning were forgotten by the Indians; the smoke of his peace-pipe had been blown away by the four winds, and the red men smeared their bodies with new war-paint, as they had done in days of old. But, brave as they were, none of them dared to hunt the monster bear, who was the terror of the nations of the earth. He would rise from his winter sleep and bring the fear of death into the villages, and he would come like a great shadow in the night to kill and to destroy. Year by year the great bear became bolder, and year by year the number of his victims had increased until the mighty Mudjekeewis, bravest of all the early Indians, grew into manhood.

Although Mudjekeewis was so strong that all his enemies were afraid of him, he did not love the war-path, for he alone remembered the warning of the great Manito; and as he wished to be a hero, and yet to do no harm to his fellow men, he decided to hunt and kill the great bear of the mountains, and to take the magic belt of shining shells called wampum that the great bear wore about his neck. Mudjekeewis told this to the Indians, and one and all they shouted: "Honor be to Mudjekeewis!"

For a weapon he took a huge war-club, made of rock and the trunk of a tough young pine, and all alone he went into the Northland to the home of Mishe Mokwa. Many days he hunted, for the great bear knew of his coming, and the monster's savage heart felt fear for the first time; but at last, after a long search, Mudjekeewis heard a sound like far-off thunder, that rose and fell and rose again until the echoes all around were rumbling, and he knew the sound to be the heavy breathing of the giant bear, who slept. Softly Mudjekeewis stole upon him.

The great bear was sprawled upon the mountain, so huge that his fore-quarters rose above the tallest boulders, and on his rough and wrinkled hide the belt of wampum shone like a string of jewels. Still he slept; and Mudjekeewis, almost frightened by the long red talons and the mighty arms and fore-paws of the monster, drew the shining wampum softly over the closed eyes and over the grim muzzle of the bear, whose heavy breathing was hot upon his hands.

Then Mudjekeewis gripped his club and swung it high above his head, shouting his war-cry in a terrible voice, and he struck the great bear on the forehead a blow that would have split the rocks on which the monster slept. The great bear rose and staggered forward, but his senses reeled and his legs trembled beneath him. Stunned, he sat upon his haunches, and from his mighty chest and throat came a little whimpering cry like the crying of a woman. Mudjekeewis laughed at the great bear, and raising his war-club once again, he broke the great bear's skull as ice is broken in winter. He put on the belt of wampum and returned to his own people, who were proud of him and cried out with one voice that the West-wind should be given him to rule. Thenceforth he was known as Kabeyun, father of the winds and ruler of the air.

Kabeyun had three sons, to whom he gave the three remaining winds of heaven. To Wabun he gave the steady East-wind, fresh and damp with the air of the ocean; to the lazy Shawondasee he gave the scented breezes of the south, and to the cruel Kabibonokka he gave the icy gusts and storm-blasts of the Northland.

Wabun, the young and beautiful, ruled the morning, and would fly from hill to hill and plain to plain awakening the world. When he came with the dew of early dawn upon his shoulders the wild fowl would splash amid the marshes and the lakes and rivers wrinkle into life. The squirrels would begin to chatter in the tree-tops, the moose would crash through the thicket, and the smoke would rise from a thousand wigwams.

And yet, although the birds never sang so gayly as when Wabun was in the air, and the flowers never smelled so sweet as when Wabun blew upon their petals, he was not happy, for he lived alone in heaven. But one morning, when he sprang from the cloud bank where he had lain through the night, and when he was passing over a yet unawakened village, Wabun saw a maiden picking rushes from the brink of a river, and as he passed above her she looked up with eyes as blue as two blue lakes. Every morning she waited for him by the river bank, and Wabun loved the beautiful maiden. So he came down to earth and he wooed her, wrapped her in his robe of crimson till he changed her to a star and he bore her high into the heavens. There they may be seen always together, Wabun and the pure, bright star he loves—the Star of Morning.

But his brother, the fierce and cruel Kabibonokka, lived among the eternal ice caves and the snowdrifts of the north. He would whisk away the leaves in autumn and send the sleet through the naked forest; he would drive the wild fowl swiftly to the south and rush through the woods after them, roaring and rattling the branches. He would bind the lakes and rivers in the keenest, hardest ice, and make them hum and sing beneath him as he whirled along beneath the stars, and he would cause great floes and icebergs to creak and groan and grind together in agony of cold.

Once Kabibonokka was rushing southward after the departing wild fowl, when he saw a figure on the frozen moorland. It was Shingebis, the diver, who had stayed in the country of the North-wind long after his tribe had gone away, and Shingebis was making ready to pass the winter there in spite of Kabibonokka and his gusty anger. He was dragging strings of fish to his winter lodge—enough to last him until spring should set the rivers free and fill the air once more with wild fowl and the waters with returning salmon.

What did Shingebis care for the anger of Kabibonokka? He had four great logs to burn as firewood (one for each moon of the winter), and he stretched himself before the blazing fire and ate and laughed and sang as merrily as if the sun were warm and bright without his cheery wigwam.

"Ho," cried Kabibonokka, "I will rush upon him! I will shake his lodge to pieces! I will scatter his bright fire and drive him far to the south!" And in the night Kabibonokka piled the snowdrifts high about the lodge of Shingebis, and shook the lodge-pole and wailed around the smoke-flue until the flames flared and the ashes were scattered on the floor. But Shingebis cared not at all. He merely turned the log until it burned more brightly, and laughed and sang as he had done before, only a little louder: "O Kabibonokka, you are but my fellow-mortal!"

"I will freeze him with my bitter breath!" roared Kabibonokka; "I will turn him to a block of ice," and he burst into the lodge of Shingebis. But although Shingebis knew by the sudden coldness on his back that Kabibonokka stood beside him, he did not even turn his head, but blew upon the embers, struck the coals and made the sparks flicker up the smoke-flue, while he laughed and sang over and over again: "O Kabibonokka, you are but my fellow-mortal!"

Drops of sweat trickled down Kabibonokka's forehead, and his limbs grew hot and moist and commenced to melt away. From his snow-sprinkled locks the water dripped as from the melting icicles in spring, and the steam rose from his shoulders. He rushed from the lodge and howled upon the moorland; for he could not bear the heat and the merry laughter and the singing of Shingebis, the diver.

"Come out and wrestle with me!" cried Kabibonokka. "Come and meet me face to face upon the moorland!" And he stamped upon the ice and made it thicker; breathed upon the snow and made it harder; raged upon the frozen marshes against Shingebis, and the warm, merry fire that had driven him away.

Then Shingebis, the diver, left his lodge and all the warmth and light that was in it, and he wrestled all night long on the marshes with Kabibonokka, until the North-wind's frozen grasp became more feeble and his strength was gone. And Kabibonokka rose from the fight and fled from Shingebis far away into the very heart of his frozen kingdom in the north.

Shawondasee, the lazy one, ruler of the South-wind, had his kingdom in the land of warmth and pleasure of the sunlit tropics. The smoke of his pipe would fill the air with a dreamy haze that caused the grapes and melons to swell into delicious ripeness. He breathed upon the fields until they yielded rich tobacco; he dropped soft and starry blossoms on the meadows and filled the shaded woods with the singing of a hundred different birds.

How the wild rose and the shy arbutus and the lily, sweet and languid, loved the idle Shawondasee! How the frost-weary and withered earth would melt and mellow at his sunny touch! Happy Shawondasee! In all his life he had a single sorrow—just one sleepy little sting of pain. He had seen a maiden clad in purest green, with hair as yellow as the bright breast of the oriole, and she stood and nodded at him from the prairie toward the north. But Shawondasee, although he loved the bright-haired maiden and longed for her until he filled the air with sighs of tenderness, was so lazy and listless that he never sought to win her love. Never did he rouse himself and tell her of his passion, but he stayed far to the southward, and murmured half asleep among the palm-trees as he dreamed of the bright maiden.

One morning, when he awoke and gazed as usual toward the north, he saw that the beautiful golden hair of the maiden had become as white as snow, and Shawondasee cried out in his sorrow: "Ah, my brother of the North-wind, you have robbed me of my treasure! You have stolen the bright-haired maiden, and have wooed her with your stories of the Northland!" and Shawondasee wandered through the air, sighing with passion until, lo and behold! the maiden disappeared.

Foolish Shawondasee! It was no maiden that you longed for. It was the prairie dandelion, and you puffed her away forever with your useless sighing.

III

HIAWATHA'S CHILDHOOD

NO doubt you will wonder what the stories of the Four Winds have to do with Hiawatha, and why he has not been spoken of before; but soon you will see that if you had not read these stories, you could not understand how the life of Hiawatha was different from that of any other Indian. And Hiawatha had been chosen by the great Manito to be the leader of the red men, to share their troubles and to teach them; so of course there were a great many things that took place before he was born that have to be remembered when we think of him.

In the full moon, long ago, the beautiful Nokomis was swinging in a swing of grape-vines and playing with her women, when one of them, who had always wished to do her harm, cut the swing and let Nokomis fall to earth. As she fell, she was so fair and bright that she seemed to be a star flashing downward through the air, and the Indians all cried out: "See, a star is dropping to the meadow!"

There on the meadow, among the blossoms and the grasses, a daughter was born to Nokomis, and she called her daughter Wenonah. And her daughter, who was born beneath the clear moon and the bright stars of heaven, grew into a maiden sweeter than the lilies of the prairie, lovelier than the moonlight and purer than the light of any star.

Wenonah was so beautiful that the West-wind, the mighty West-wind, Mudjekeewis, came and whispered tenderly into her ear until she loved him. But the West-wind did not love Wenonah long. He went away to his kingdom on the mountains, and after he had gone Wenonah had a son whom she named Hiawatha, the child of the West-wind. But Wenonah was so sad because the West-wind had deserted her that she died soon after Hiawatha was born, and the infant Hiawatha, without father or mother, was taken to Nokomis' wigwam, which stood beside a broad and shining lake called "The Big-Sea-Water."

There he lived and was nursed by his grandmother, Nokomis, who sang to him and rocked him in his cradle. When he cried Nokomis would say to him: "Hush, or the naked bear will get thee," and when he awoke in the night she taught him all about the stars, and showed him the spirits that we call the northern lights dance the Death-dance far in the north.

On the summer evenings, little Hiawatha would hear the pine-trees whisper to one another and the water lapping in the lake, and he would see the fire-flies twinkle in the twilight; and when he saw the moon and all the dark spots on it he asked Nokomis what they were, and she told him that a very angry warrior had once seized his grandmother and thrown her up into the sky at midnight, "right up to the moon," said Nokomis, "and that is her body that you see there."

When Hiawatha saw the rainbow, with the sun shining on it, he said: "What is that, Nokomis?" and Nokomis answered, saying: "That is the heaven of the flowers, where all the flowers that fade on the earth blossom once again." And when Hiawatha heard the owls hooting through the night he asked Nokomis: "What are those?" And Nokomis answered: "Those are the owls and the owlets, talking to each other in their native language."

Then Hiawatha learned the language of all the birds of the air, all about their nests, how they learned to fly and where they went in winter; and he learned so much that he could talk to them just as if he were a bird himself. He learned the language of all the beasts of the forest, and they told him all their secrets. The beavers showed him how they built their houses, the squirrels took him to the places where they hid their acorns, and the rabbits told him why they were so timid. Hiawatha talked with all the animals that he met, and he called them "Hiawatha's brothers."

Nokomis had a friend called Iagoo the Boaster, because he told so many stories about great deeds that he had never done, and this Iagoo once made a bow for Hiawatha, and said to him: "Take this bow, and go into the forest hunting. Kill a fine roebuck and bring us back his horns." So Hiawatha went into the forest all alone with his bow and arrows, and because he knew the language of the wild things he could tell what all the birds and animals were saying to him.

"Do not shoot us, Hiawatha!" said the robins; and the squirrels scrambled in fright up the trunks of the trees, coughing and chattering: "Do not shoot us, Hiawatha!" But for once Hiawatha did not care or even hear what the birds and beasts were saying to him.

At last he saw the tracks of the red deer, and he followed them to the river bank, where he hid among the bushes and waited until two antlers rose above the thicket and a fine buck stepped out into the path and snuffed the wind. Hiawatha's heart beat quickly and he rose to one knee and aimed his arrow. "Twang!" went the bowstring, and the buck leaped high into the air and fell down dead, with the arrow in his heart. Hiawatha dragged the buck that he had killed back to the wigwam of Nokomis, and Nokomis and Iagoo were much pleased. From the buck-skin they made a fine cloak for Hiawatha; they hung up the antlers in the wigwam, and invited everybody in the village to a feast of deer's flesh. And the Indians all came and feasted, and called Hiawatha "Strong Heart."

IV

HIAWATHA AND MUDJEKEEWIS

THE years passed, and Hiawatha grew from a child into a strong and active man. He was so wise that the old men knew far less than he, and often asked him for advice, and he was such a fine hunter that he never missed his aim. He was so swift of foot that he could shoot an arrow and catch it in its flight or let it fall behind him; he was so strong that he could shoot ten arrows up into the air, and the last of them would leave his bow before the first had fallen to the ground. He had magic mittens made of deer-skin, and when he wore them on his hands he could break the rocks with them and grind the pieces into powder; he had magic moccasins also—shoes made of deer-skin that he tied about his feet, and when he put on these he could take a mile at every step.

Hiawatha thought a great deal about his father, Mudjekeewis, and often plagued Nokomis with questions about him, until at last she told Hiawatha how his mother had loved Mudjekeewis, who left her to die of sorrow; and Hiawatha was so angry when he heard the story that his heart felt like a coal of fire. He said to Nokomis: "I will talk with Mudjekeewis, my father, and to find him I will go to the Land of the Sunset, where he has his kingdom."

So Hiawatha dressed himself for travel and armed himself with bow and a war-club, took his magic mittens and his magic moccasins, and set out all alone to travel to the kingdom of the West-wind. And although Nokomis called after him and begged him to turn back, he would not listen to her, but went away into the forest.

For days and days he traveled. He passed the Mississippi River; he crossed the prairies where the buffaloes were herding, and when he came to the Rocky Mountains, where the panther and the grizzly bear have their homes, he reached the Land of the Sunset, and the kingdom of the West-wind. There he found his father, Mudjekeewis.

When Hiawatha saw his father he was as nearly afraid as he had ever been in his life, for his father's cloudy hair tossed and waved in the air and flashed like the star we call the comet, trailing long streams of fire through the sky. But when Mudjekeewis saw what a strong and handsome man his son had grown to be, he was proud and happy; for he knew that Hiawatha had all of his own early strength and all the beauty of the dead Wenonah.

"Welcome, my son," said Mudjekeewis, "to the kingdom of the West-wind. I have waited for you many years, and have grown very lonely." And Mudjekeewis and Hiawatha talked long together; but all the while Hiawatha was thinking of his dead mother and the wrong that had been done to her, and he became more and more angry.

He hid his anger, however, and listened to what Mudjekeewis told him, and Mudjekeewis boasted of his own early bravery and of his body that was so tough that nobody could do him any harm. "Can nothing hurt you?" asked Hiawatha, and Mudjekeewis said: "Nothing but the black rock yonder." Then he smiled at Hiawatha and said: "Is there anything that can harm you, my son?" And Hiawatha, who did not wish Mudjekeewis to know that nothing in the world could do him injury, told him that only the bulrush had such power.

Then they talked about other things—of Hiawatha's brothers who ruled the winds, Wabun and Shawondasee and Kabibonokka, and about the beautiful Wenonah, Hiawatha's mother. And Hiawatha cried out then in fury: "Father though you be, you killed Wenonah!" And he struck with his magic mittens the black rock, broke it into pieces, and threw them at Mudjekeewis; but Mudjekeewis blew them back with his breath, and remembering what Hiawatha said about the bulrushes he tore them up from the mud, roots and all, and used them as a whip to lash his son.

Thus began the fearful fight between Hiawatha and his father, Mudjekeewis. The eagle left his nest and circled in the air above them as they fought; the bulrush bent and waved like a tall tree in a storm, and great pieces of the black rock crashed upon the earth. Three days the fight continued, and Mudjekeewis was driven back—back to the end of the world, where the sun drops down into the empty places every evening.

"Stop!" cried Mudjekeewis, "stop, Hiawatha! You cannot kill me. I have put you to this trial to learn how brave you are. Now I will give you a great prize. Go back to your home and people, and kill all the monsters, and all the giants and the serpents, as I killed the great bear when I was young. And at last when Death draws near you, and his awful eyes glare on you from the darkness, I will give you a part of my kingdom and you shall be ruler of the North-west wind."

Then the battle ended long ago among the mountains; and if you do not believe this story, go there and see for yourself that the bulrush grows by the ponds and rivers, and that the pieces of the black rock are scattered all through the valleys, where they fell after Hiawatha had thrown them at his father.

Hiawatha started homeward, with all the anger taken from his heart. Only once upon his way he stopped and bought the heads of arrows from an old Arrow-maker who lived in the land of the Indians called Dacotahs. The old Arrow-maker had a daughter, whose laugh was as musical as the voice of the waterfall by which she lived, and Hiawatha named her by the name of the rushing waterfall—"Minnehaha"—Laughing Water. When he reached his native village, all he told to Nokomis was of the battle with his father. Of the arrows and the lovely maiden, Minnehaha, he did not say a word.

V

HIAWATHA'S FASTING

THE time came when Hiawatha felt that he must show the tribes of Indians that he would do them some great service, and he went alone into the forest to fast and pray, and see if he could not learn how to help his fellow-men and make them happy. In the forest he built a wigwam, where nobody might disturb him, and he went without food for seven nights and seven days. The first day, he walked in the forest; and when he saw the hare leap into the thicket and the deer dart away at his approach he was very sad, because he knew that if the animals of the forest should die, or go and hide where the Indians could not hunt them, the Indians would starve for want of food. "Must our lives depend on the hare and on the red deer?" asked Hiawatha, and he prayed to the Great Manito to tell him of some food that the Indians might always be able to find when they were hungry.

The next day, Hiawatha walked by the bank of the river, and saw the wild rice growing and the blueberries and the wild strawberries and the grape-vine that filled the air with pleasant odors; and he knew that when cold winter came, all this fruit would wither and the Indians would have no more of it to eat. Again he prayed to the Great Manito to tell him of some food that the Indians might enjoy in winter and summer, in autumn and in spring.

The third day that Hiawatha fasted, he was too weak to walk about the forest, and he sat by the shore of the lake and watched the yellow perch darting about in the sunny water. Far out in the middle of the lake he saw Nahma, the big sturgeon, leap into the air with a shower of spray and fall back into the water with a crash; and every now and then the pike would chase a school of minnows into the shallow water at the edges of the lake and dart among them like an arrow. And Hiawatha thought of how a hot summer might dry up the lakes and rivers and kill the fish, or drive them into such deep water that nobody could catch them; and he called out to the Great Manito, asking a third time for some food that the Indians could store away and use when there was no game in the forest, and no fruit on the river banks or in the fields, and no fish in any of the lakes and rivers.

On the fourth day that Hiawatha fasted, he was so weak from hunger that he could not even go out and sit beside the lake, but lay on his back in his wigwam and watched the rising sun burn away the mist, and he looked up into the blue sky, wondering if the Great Manito had heard his prayers and would tell him of this food that he wished so much to find. And just as the sun was sinking down behind the hills, Hiawatha saw a young man with golden hair coming through the forest toward his wigwam, and the young man wore a wonderful dress of the brightest green, with silky yellow fringes and gay tassels that waved behind him in the wind.

The young man walked right into Hiawatha's wigwam and said: "Hiawatha, my name is Mondamin, and I have been sent by the Great Manito to tell you that he has heard your prayers and will give you the food that you wish to find. But you must work hard and suffer a great deal before this food is given you, and you must now come out of your wigwam and wrestle with me in the forest."

Then Hiawatha rose from his bed of leaves and branches, but he was so weak that it was all he could do to follow Mondamin from the wigwam. He wrestled with Mondamin, and as soon as he touched him his strength began to return. They wrestled for a long time and at last Mondamin said: "It is enough. You have wrestled bravely, Hiawatha. To-morrow I will come again and wrestle with you." He vanished, and Hiawatha could not tell whether he had sunk into the ground or disappeared into the air.

"DEAD HE LAY THERE IN THE SUNSET"—*Page 153*

9

On the next day, when the sun was setting, Mondamin came again to wrestle with Hiawatha, and the day after that he came also and they wrestled even longer than before. Then Mondamin smiled at Hiawatha and said to him: "Three times, O Hiawatha, you have bravely wrestled with me. To-morrow I shall wrestle with you once again, and you will overcome me and throw me to the earth and I shall seem to be dead. Then, when I am lying still and limp on the ground, do you take off my gay clothes and bury me where we have wrestled. And you must make the ground above the place where I am buried soft and light, and take good care that weeds do not grow there and that ravens do not come there to disturb me, until at last I rise again from the ground more beautiful than ever."

True to his word, Mondamin came at sunset of the next day, and he and Hiawatha wrestled together for the last time. They wrestled after evening had come upon them, until at last Hiawatha threw Mondamin to the ground, who lay there as if dead.

Then Hiawatha took off all the gay green clothes that Mondamin wore, and he buried Mondamin and made the ground soft and light above the grave, just as he had been told to do. He kept the weeds from growing in the ground, and kept the ravens from coming to the place, until at last he saw a tiny little green leaf sticking up out of the grave. The little leaf grew into a large plant, taller than Hiawatha himself, and the plant had wonderful green leaves and silky yellow fringes and gay tassels that waved behind it in the wind. "It is Mondamin!" cried out Hiawatha, and he called Nokomis and Iagoo to see the wonderful plant that was to be the food that he had prayed for to the Great Manito.

They waited until autumn had turned the leaves to yellow, and made the tender kernels hard and shiny, and then they stripped the husks and gathered the ears of the wonderful Indian corn. All the Indians for miles around had a great feast and were happy, because they knew that with a little care they would have corn to eat in winter and in summer, in autumn and in spring.

VI

HIAWATHA'S FRIENDS

HIAWATHA had two good friends, whom he had chosen from all other Indians to be with him always, and whom he loved more than any living men. They were Chibiabos, the sweetest singer, and Kwasind, the strongest man in the world; and they told to Hiawatha all their secrets as he told his to them. Best of all Hiawatha loved the brave and beautiful Chibiabos, who was such a wonderful musician that when he sang people flocked from villages far and near to listen to him, and even the animals and birds left their dens and nests to hear.

Chibiabos sang so sweetly that the brook would pause in its course and murmur to him, asking him to teach its waves to sing his songs and to flow as softly as his words flowed when he was singing. The envious bluebird begged Chibiabos to teach it songs as wild and wonderful as his own; the robin tried to learn his notes of gladness, and the lonely bird of night, the whippoorwill, longed to sing as Chibiabos sang when he was sad. He could imitate all the noises of the woodland, and make them sound even sweeter than they really were, and by his singing he could force the Indians to laugh or cry or dance, just as he chose.

The mighty Kwasind was also much beloved by Hiawatha, who believed that next to wonderful songs and love and wisdom great strength was the finest thing in the world and the closest to perfect goodness; and never, in all the years that men have lived upon the earth, has there been another man so strong as Kwasind.

When he was a boy, Kwasind did not fish or play with other children, but seemed very dull and dreamy, and his father and mother thought that they were bringing up a fool. "Lazy Kwasind!" his mother said to him, "you never help me with my work. In the summer you roam through the fields and forests, doing nothing; and now that it is winter you sit beside the fire like an old woman, and leave me to break the ice for fishing and to draw the nets alone. Go out and wring them now, where they are freezing with the water that is in them; hang them up to dry in the sunshine, and show that you are worth the food that you eat and the clothes you wear on your back."

Without a word Kwasind rose from the ashes where he was sitting, left the lodge and found the nets dripping and freezing fast. He wrung them like a wisp of straw, but his fingers were so strong that he broke them in a hundred different places, and his strength was so great that he could not help breaking the nets any more than if they were tender cobwebs.

"Lazy Kwasind!" his father said to him, "you never help me in my hunting, as other young men help their fathers. You break every bow you touch, and you snap every arrow that you draw. Yet you shall come with me and bring home from the forest what I kill."

They went down to a deep and narrow valley by the side of a little brook, where the tracks of bison and of deer showed plainly in the mud; and at last they came to a place where the trunks of heavy trees were piled like a stone wall across the valley.

"We must go back," said Kwasind's father; "we can never scale those logs. They are packed so tightly that no woodchuck could get through them, and not even a squirrel could climb over the top," and the old man sat down to smoke and rest and wonder what they were going to do; but before he had finished his pipe the way lay clear, for the strong Kwasind had lifted the logs as if they were light lances, and had hurled them crashing into the depths of the forest.

"Lazy Kwasind!" shouted the young men, as they ran their races and played their games upon the meadows, "why do you stay idle while we strive with one another? Leave the rock that you are leaning on and join us. Come and wrestle with us, and see who can pitch the quoit the farthest."

Kwasind did not say a word in answer to them, but rose and slowly turned to the huge rock on which he had been leaning. He gripped it with both hands, tore it from the ground and pitched it right into the swift Pauwating River, where you can still see it in the summer months, as it towers high above the current.

Once as Kwasind with his companions was sailing down the foaming rapids of the Pauwating he saw a beaver in the water—Ahmeek, the King of Beavers—who was struggling against the savage current. Without a word, Kwasind leaped into the water and chased the beaver in and out among the whirlpools. He followed the beaver among the islands, dove after him to the bottom of the river and stayed under water so long that his companions believed him dead and cried out: "Alas, we shall see Kwasind no more! He is drowned in the whirlpool!" But Kwasind's head showed at last above the water and he swam ashore, carrying the King of Beavers dead upon his shoulders.

These were the sort of men that Hiawatha chose to be his friends.

VII

HIAWATHA'S SAILING

ONCE Hiawatha was sitting alone beside the swift and mighty river Taquamenaw, and he longed for a canoe with which he might explore the river from bank to bank, and learn to know all its rapids and its shallows. And Hiawatha set about building himself a canoe such as he needed, and he called upon the forest to give him aid:

"Give me your bark, O Birch Tree!" cried Hiawatha; "I will build me a light canoe for sailing that shall float upon the river like a yellow leaf in autumn. Lay aside your cloak, O Birch Tree, for the summer time is coming." And the birch tree sighed and rustled in the breeze, murmuring sadly: "Take my cloak, O Hiawatha!"

With his knife Hiawatha cut around the trunk of the birch-tree just beneath the branches until the sap came oozing forth; and he also cut the bark around the tree-trunk just above the roots. He slashed the bark from top to bottom, raised it with wooden wedges and stripped it from the trunk of the tree without a crack in all its golden surface.

"Give me your boughs, O Cedar!" cried Hiawatha. "Give me your strong and pliant branches, to make my canoe firmer and tougher beneath me." Through all the branches of the cedar there swept a noise as if somebody were crying with horror, but the tree at last bent downward and whispered: "Take my boughs, O Hiawatha."

He cut down the boughs of the cedar and made them into a framework with the shape of two bows bent together, and he covered this framework with the rich and yellow bark.

"Give me your roots, O Larch Tree!" cried Hiawatha, "to bind the ends of my canoe together, that the water may not enter and the river may not wet me!" The larch-tree shivered in the air and touched Hiawatha's forehead with its tassels, sighing: "Take them, take them!" as he tore the fibres from the earth. With the tough roots he sewed the ends of his canoe together and bound the bark tightly to the framework, and his canoe became light and graceful in shape. He took the balsam and pitch of the fir-tree and smeared the seams so that no water might ooze in, and he asked for the quills of Kagh, the hedgehog, to make a necklace and two stars for his canoe.

Thus did Hiawatha build his birch canoe, and all the life and magic of the forest was held in it; for it had all the lightness of the bark of the birch-tree, all the toughness of the boughs of the cedar, and it danced and floated on the river as lightly as a yellow leaf.

Hiawatha did not have any paddles for his canoe, and he needed none, for he could guide it by merely wishing that it should turn to the right or to the left. The canoe would move in whatever direction he chose, and would glide over the water swiftly or slowly just as he desired. All Hiawatha had to do was to sit still and think where he cared to have it take him. Never was there such a wonderful craft before.

Then Hiawatha called to Kwasind, and asked for help in clearing away all the sunken logs and all the rocks, and sandbars in the river-bed, and he and Kwasind traveled down the whole length of the river. Kwasind swam and dove like a beaver, tugging at sunken logs, scooping out the sandbars with his hands, kicking the boulders out of the stream and digging away all the snags and tangles. They went back and forth and up and down the river, Kwasind working just as hard as he was able, and Hiawatha showing him where he could find new logs and rocks, and sandbars to remove, until together they made the channel safe and regular all the way from where the river rose among the mountains in little springs to where it emptied a wide and rolling sheet of water into the bay of Taquamenaw.

VIII

HIAWATHA'S FISHING

IN his wonderful canoe, Hiawatha sailed over the shining Big-Sea-Water to go fishing and to catch with his fishing-line made of cedar no other than the very King of Fishes—Nahma, the big sturgeon. All alone Hiawatha sailed over the lake, but on the bow of his canoe sat a squirrel, frisking and chattering at the thought of all the wonderful sport that he was going to see. Through the calm, clear water Hiawatha saw the fishes swimming to and fro. First he saw the yellow perch that shone like a sunbeam; then he saw the crawfish moving along the sandy bottom of the lake, and at last he saw a great blue shape that swept the sand floor with its mighty tail and waved its huge fins lazily backward and forward, and Hiawatha knew that this monster was Nahma, the Sturgeon, King of all the Fishes.

"Take my bait!" shouted Hiawatha, dropping his line of cedar into the calm water. "Come up and take my bait, O Nahma, King of Fishes!" But the great fish did not move, although Hiawatha shouted to him over and over again. At last, however, Nahma began to grow tired of the endless shouting, and he said to Maskenozha, the pike: "Take the bait of this rude fellow, Hiawatha, and break his line."

Hiawatha felt the fishing-line tighten with a snap, and as he pulled it in, Maskenozha, the pike, tugged so hard that the canoe stood almost on end, with the squirrel perched on the top; but when Hiawatha saw what fish it was that had taken his bait he was full of scorn and shouted: "Shame upon you! You are not the King of Fishes; you are only the pike, Maskenozha!" and the pike let go of Hiawatha's line and sank back to the bottom, very much ashamed.

Then Nahma said to the sunfish, Ugudwash: "Take Hiawatha's bait, and break his line! I am tired of his shouting and his boasting," and the sunfish rose up through the water like a great white moon. It seized Hiawatha's line and struggled so that the canoe made a whirlpool in the water and rocked until the waves it made splashed upon the beaches at the rim of the lake; but when Hiawatha saw the fish he was very angry and shouted out again: "Oh shame upon you! You are the sunfish, Ugudwash, and you come when I call for Nahma, King of Fishes!" and the sunfish let go of Hiawatha's line and sank to the bottom, where he hid among the lily stems.

Then Nahma, the great sturgeon, heard Hiawatha shouting at him once again, and furious he rose with a swirl to the top of the water; leaped in the air, scattering the spray on every side, and opening his huge jaws he made a rush at the canoe and swallowed Hiawatha, canoe and all.

Into the dark cave of Nahma's giant maw, Hiawatha in his canoe plunged headlong, as a log rushes down a roaring river in the springtime. At first he was frightened, for it was so inky black that he could not see his hand before his face; but at last he felt a great heart beating in the darkness, and he clenched his fist and struck the giant heart with all his strength. As he struck it, he felt Nahma tremble all over, and he heard the water gurgle as the great fish rushed through it trying to breathe, and Hiawatha struck the mighty heart yet another heavy blow.

Then he dragged his canoe crosswise, so that he might not be thrown from the belly of the great fish and be drowned in the swirling water where Nahma was fighting for life, and the little squirrel helped Hiawatha drag his canoe into safety and tugged and pulled bravely at Hiawatha's side. Hiawatha was grateful to the little squirrel, and told him that for a reward the boys should always call him Adjidaumo, which means "tail-in-the-air," and the little squirrel was much pleased.

At last everything became quiet, and Nahma, the great sturgeon, lay dead and drifted on the surface of the water to the shore, where Hiawatha heard him grate upon the pebbles. There was a great screaming and flapping of wings outside, and finally a gleam of light shone to the place where Hiawatha was sitting, and he could see the glittering eyes of the sea-gulls, who had crawled into the open mouth of Nahma and were peering down his gullet. Hiawatha called out to them: "O my Brothers, the Sea-Gulls, I have killed the great King of Fishes, Nahma, the sturgeon. Scratch and tear with your beaks and claws until the opening becomes wider and you can set me free from this dark prison! Do this, and men shall always call you Kayoshk, the sea-gulls, the Noble Scratchers."

The sea-gulls set to work with a will, and scratched and tore at Nahma's ribs until there was an opening wide enough for Hiawatha and the squirrel to step through and to drag the canoe out after them. Hiawatha called Nokomis, pointed to the body of the sturgeon and said: "See, Nokomis, I have killed Nahma, the King of Fishes, and the sea-gulls feed upon him. You must not drive them away, for they saved me from great danger; but when they fly back to their nests at sunset, do you bring your pots and kettles and make from Nahma's flesh enough oil to last us through the winter."

Nokomis waited until sunset, when the sea-gulls had flown back to their homes in the marshes, and she set to work with all her pots and kettles to make yellow oil from the flesh of Nahma. She worked all night long until the sun rose again and the sea-gulls came back screeching and screaming for their breakfast; and for three days and three nights the sea-gulls and Nokomis took turns in stripping the greasy flesh of Nahma from his ribs, until nothing was left. Then the sea-gulls flew away for good and all, Nokomis poured her oil into great jars, and on the sand was only the bare skeleton of Nahma, who had once been the biggest and the strongest fish that ever swam.

IX

HIAWATHA AND THE PEARL-FEATHER

ONCE Nokomis was standing with Hiawatha beside her upon the shore of the Big-Sea-Water, watching the sunset, and she pointed to the west, and said to Hiawatha: "There is the dwelling of the Pearl-Feather, the great wizard who is guarded by the fiery snakes that coil and play together in the black pitch-water. You can see them now." And Hiawatha beheld the fiery snakes twist and wriggle in the black water and coil and uncoil themselves in play. Nokomis went on: "The great wizard killed my father, who had come down from the moon to find me. He killed him by wicked spells and by sly cunning, and now he sends the rank mist of marshes and the deadly fog that brings sickness and death among our people. Take your bow, Hiawatha," said Nokomis, "and your war-club and your magic mittens. Take the oil of the sturgeon, Nahma, so that your canoe may glide easily through the sticky black pitch-water, and go and kill this great wizard. Save our people from the fever that he breathes at them across the marshes, and punish him for my father's death."

Swiftly Hiawatha took his war-club and his arrows and his magic mittens, launched his birch canoe upon the water and cried: "O Birch Canoe, leap forward where you see the snakes that play in the black pitch-water. Leap forward swiftly, O my Birch Canoe, while I sing my war-song," and the canoe darted forward like a live thing until it reached the spot where the fiery serpents were sporting in the water.

"Out of my way, O serpents!" cried Hiawatha, "out of my way and let me go to fight with Pearl-Feather, the awful wizard!" But the serpents only hissed and answered: "Go back, Coward; go back to old Nokomis, Faint-heart!"

Then Hiawatha took his bow and sent his arrows singing among the serpents, and at every shot one of them was killed, until they all lay dead upon the water.

"Onward, my Birch Canoe!" cried Hiawatha; "onward to the home of the great wizard!" and the canoe darted forward once again.

It was a strange, strange place that Hiawatha had entered with his birch canoe! The water was as black as ink, and on the shores of the lake dead men lit fires that twinkled in the darkness like the eyes of a wicked old witch. Awful shrieks and whistling echoed over the water, and the heron flapped about the marshes to tell all the evil beings who lived there that Hiawatha was coming to fight with the great wizard.

Hiawatha sailed over this dismal lake all night long, and at last, when the sun rose, he saw on the shore in front of him the wigwam of the great magician, Pearl-Feather. The canoe darted ahead faster and faster until it grated on the beach, and Hiawatha fitted an arrow to his bowstring and sent it hissing into the open doorway of the wigwam.

"Come out and fight me, Pearl-Feather!" cried Hiawatha; "come out and fight me if you dare!"

Then Pearl-Feather stepped out of his wigwam and stood in the open before Hiawatha. He was painted red and yellow and blue and was terrible to see. In his hand was a heavy war-club, and he wore a shirt of shining wampum that would keep out an arrow and break the force of any blow.

"Well do I know you, Hiawatha!" shouted Pearl-Feather in a deep and awful voice. "Go back to Nokomis, coward that you are; for if you stay here, I will kill you as I killed her father."

"Words are not as sharp as arrows," answered Hiawatha, bending his bow.

Then began a battle even more terrible than the one among the mountains when Hiawatha fought with Mudjekeewis, and it lasted all one summer's day. For Hiawatha's arrows could not pierce Pearl-Feather's shirt of wampum, and he could not break it with the blows of his magic mittens.

At sunset Hiawatha was so weary that he leaned on his bow to rest. His heavy war-club was broken, his magic mittens were torn to pieces, and he had only three arrows left. "Alas," sighed Hiawatha, "the great magician is too strong for me!"

Suddenly, from the branches of the tree nearest him, he heard the woodpecker calling to him: "Hiawatha, Hiawatha," said the woodpecker, "aim your arrows at the tuft of hair on Pearl-Feather's head. Aim them at the roots of his long black hair, for there alone can you do him any harm." Just then Pearl-Feather stooped to pick up a big stone to throw at Hiawatha, who bent his bow and struck Pearl-Feather with an arrow right on the top of the head. Pearl-Feather staggered forward like a wounded buffalo. "Twang!" went the bowstring again, and the wizard's knees trembled beneath him, for the second arrow had struck in the same spot as the first and had made the wound much deeper. A third arrow followed swiftly, and Pearl-Feather saw the eyes of Death glare at him from the darkness, and he fell forward on his face right at the feet of Hiawatha and lay there dead.

Then Hiawatha called the woodpecker to him, and as a mark of gratitude he stained the tuft of feathers on the woodpecker's head with the blood of the dead Pearl-Feather, and the woodpecker wears his tuft of blood-red feathers to this day.

Hiawatha took the shirt of wampum from the dead wizard as a sign of victory, and from Pearl-Feather's wigwam he carried all the skins and furs and arrows that he could find, and they were many. He loaded his canoe with them and sped homeward over the pitch-water, past the dead bodies of the fiery serpents until he saw Chibiabos and Kwasind and Nokomis waiting for him on the shore. All the Indians assembled and gave a feast in Hiawatha's honor, and they sang and danced for joy because the great wizard would never again send sickness and death among them. And Hiawatha took the red crest of the woodpecker to decorate his pipe, for he knew that to the woodpecker his victory was due.

X

HIAWATHA'S WOOING

"WOMAN is to man as the cord is to the bow," thought Hiawatha. "She bends him, yet obeys him; she draws him, yet she follows. Each is useless without the other." Hiawatha was dreaming of the lovely maiden, Minnehaha, whom he had seen in the country of the Dacotahs.

"Do not wed a stranger, Hiawatha," warned the old Nokomis; "do not search in the east or in the west to win a bride. Take a maid of your own people, for the homely daughter of a neighbor is like the pleasant fire on the hearth-stone, while the stranger is cold and distant, like the starlight or the light of the pale moon."

But Hiawatha only smiled and answered: "Dear Nokomis, the fire on the hearth-stone is indeed pleasant and warm, but I love the starlight and the moonlight better."

"Do not bring home an idle woman," said old Nokomis, "bring not home a maiden who is unskilled with the needle and will neither cook nor sew!" And Hiawatha answered: "Good Nokomis, in the land of the Dacotahs lives the daughter of an Arrow-maker, and she is the most beautiful of all the women in the world. Her name is Minnehaha, and I will bring her home to do your bidding and to be your firelight, your moonlight, and your starlight, all in one."

"Ah, Hiawatha," warned Nokomis, "bring not home a maid of the Dacotahs! The Dacotahs are fierce and cruel and there is often war between our tribe and theirs." Hiawatha laughed and answered: "I will wed a maid of the Dacotahs, and old wars shall be forgotten in a new and lasting peace that shall make the two tribes friends forevermore. For this alone would I wed the lovely Laughing Water if there were no other reason."

Hiawatha left his wigwam for the home of the old Arrow-maker, and he ran through the forest as lightly as the wind, until he heard the clear voice of the Falls of Minnehaha.

At the sunny edges of the forest a herd of deer were feeding, and they did not see the swift-footed runner until he sent a hissing arrow among them that killed a roebuck. Without pausing, Hiawatha caught up the deer and swung it to his shoulder, running forward until he came to the home of the aged Arrow-maker.

The old man was sitting in the doorway of his wigwam, and at his side were all his tools and all the arrows he was making. At his side, also, was the lovely Minnehaha, weaving mats of reeds and water-rushes, and the old man and the young maiden sat together in the pleasant contrast of age and youth, the one thinking of the past, the other dreaming of the future.

The old man was thinking of the days when with such arrows as he now was making he had killed deer and bison, and had shot the wild goose on the wing. He remembered the great war-parties that came to buy his arrows, and how they could not fight unless he had arrow-*heads to sell. Alas, such days were over, he thought sadly, and no such splendid warriors were left on earth.

The maiden was dreaming of a tall, handsome hunter, who had come one morning when the year was young to purchase arrows of her father. He had rested in their wigwam, lingered and looked back as he was leaving, and her father had praised his courage and his wisdom. Would the hunter ever come again in search of arrows, thought the lovely Minnehaha, and the rushes she was weaving lay unfingered in her lap.

Just then they heard a rustle and swift footsteps in the thicket, and Hiawatha with the deer upon his shoulders and a glow upon his cheek and forehead stood before them in the sunlight.

"Welcome, Hiawatha," said the old Arrow-maker in a grave but friendly tone, and Minnehaha's light voice echoed the deep one of her father, saying: "Welcome, Hiawatha."

Together the old Arrow-maker and Hiawatha entered the wigwam, and Minnehaha laid aside her mat of rushes and brought them food and drink in vessels of earth and bowls of basswood. Yet she did not say a word while she was serving them, but listened as if in a dream to what Hiawatha told her father about Nokomis and Chibiabos and the strong man, Kwasind, and the happiness and peace of his own people, the Ojibways. Hiawatha finished his words by saying very slowly: "That this peace may always be among us and our tribes become as brothers to each other, give me the hand of your daughter, Minnehaha, the loveliest of women."

"PLEASANT WAS THE JOURNEY HOMEWARD"—*Page 199*

The aged Arrow-maker paused before he answered, looked proudly at Hiawatha and lovingly at his daughter, and then said:

"You may have her if she wishes it. Speak, Minnehaha, and let us know your will."

The lovely Minnehaha seemed more beautiful than ever as she looked first at Hiawatha and then at her old father. Softly she took the seat beside Hiawatha, blushing as she answered: "I will follow you, my husband."

Thus did Hiawatha win the daughter of the ancient Arrow-maker. Together he and his bride left the wigwam hand in hand and went away over the meadows, while the old Arrow-maker with shaded eyes gazed after them and called out sadly: "Good-bye, Minnehaha! Good-bye my lovely daughter!"

They walked together through the sunlit forest, and all the birds and animals gazed at them from among the leaves and branches.

When they came to swift rivers, Hiawatha lifted Minnehaha and carried her across, and in his strong arms she seemed lighter than a willow-leaf or the plume upon his headgear. At night he cleared away the thicket and built a lodge of branches; he made a bed of hemlock boughs and kindled a fire of pine-cones before the doorway, and Adjidaumo, the squirrel, climbed down from his nest and kept watch, while the two lovers slept in their lodge beneath the stars.

XI

HIAWATHA'S WEDDING FEAST

A GREAT feast was prepared by Hiawatha to celebrate his wedding. That the feast might be one of joy and gladness, the sweet singer Chibiabos sang his love-songs; that it might be merry, the handsome Pau-Puk-Keewis danced his liveliest dances; and to make the wedding guests even more content, Iagoo, the great boaster, told them a wonderful story. Oh, but it was a splendid feast that Nokomis prepared at the bidding of Hiawatha! She sent messengers with willow-wands through all the village as a sign that all Ojibways were invited, and the wedding guests wore their very brightest garments—rich fur robes and wampum-belts, beads of many colors, paint and feathers and gay tassels. All the bowls at the feast were made of white and shining basswood; all the spoons were made of bison horn, as black as ink and polished until the black was as bright as silver, and the Indians feasted on the flesh of the sturgeon and the pike, on buffalo marrow and the hump of the bison and the haunch of the red deer. They ate pounded meat called pemican and the wild rice that grew by the river-bank and golden-yellow cakes of Indian corn. It was a feast indeed!

But the kind host Hiawatha did not take a mouthful of all this tempting food. Neither did Minnehaha nor Nokomis, but all three waited on their guests and served them carefully until their wants were generously satisfied. When all had finished, old Nokomis filled from an ample otter pouch the red stone pipes with fragrant tobacco of the south, and when the blue smoke was rising freely she said: "O Pau-Puk-Keewis, dance your merry Beggar's Dance to please us, so the time may pass more pleasantly and our guests may be more gay."

Pau-Puk-Keewis rose and stood amid the guests. He wore a white shirt of doeskin, fringed with ermine and covered with beads of wampum. He wore deerskin leggings, also fringed with ermine and with quills of Kagh, the hedgehog. On his feet were buck-skin moccasins, richly embroidered, and red foxes' tails to flourish while he danced were fastened to the heels. A snowy plume of swan's down floated over his head, and he carried a gay fan in one hand and a pipe with tassels in the other.

All the warriors disliked Pau-Puk-Keewis, and called him coward and idler; but he cared not at all, because he was so handsome that all the women and the maidens loved him. To the sound of drums and flutes and singing voices Pau-Puk-Keewis now began the Dance of Beggars.

First he danced with slow steps and stately motion in and out of the shadows and the sunshine, gliding like a panther among the pine-trees; but his steps became faster and faster and wilder and wilder, until the wind and dust swept around him as he danced. Time after time he leaped over the heads of the assembled guests and rushed around the wigwam, and at last he sped along the shore of the Big-Sea-Water, stamping on the sand and tossing it furiously in the air, until the wind had become a whirlwind and the sand was blown in great drifts like snowdrifts all over the shore.

There they have stayed until this day, the great Sand Hills of the Nagow Wudjoo.

When the Beggar's Dance was over, Pau-Puk-Keewis returned and sat down laughing among the guests and fanned himself as calmly as if he had not stirred from his seat, while all the guests cried out: "Sing to us, Chibiabos, sing your love songs!" and Hiawatha and Nokomis said: "Yes, sing, Chibiabos, that our guests may enjoy themselves all the more, and our feast may pass more gayly!"

Chibiabos rose, and his wonderful voice swelled all the echoes of the forest, until the streams paused in their courses, and the listening beavers came to the surface of the water so that they might hear. He sang so sweetly that his voice caused the pine-trees to quiver as if a wind were passing through them, and strange sounds seemed to run along the earth. All the Indians were spellbound by his singing, and sat as if they had been turned to stone. Even the smoke ceased to rise from their pipes while Chibiabos sang, but when he had ended they shouted with joy and praised him in loud voices.

Iagoo, the mighty boaster, alone did not join in the roar of praise, for he was jealous of Chibiabos, and longed to tell one of his great stories to the Indians. When Iagoo heard of any adventure he always told of a greater one that had happened to himself, and to listen to him, you would think that nobody was such a mighty hunter and nobody was such a valiant fighter as he. If you would only believe him, you would learn nobody had ever shot an arrow half so far as he had, that nobody could run so fast, or dive so deep, or leap so high, and that nobody in the wide world had ever seen so many wonders as the brave, great, and wonderful Iagoo.

This was the reason that his name had become a byword among the Indians; and whenever a hunter spoke too highly of his own deeds, or a warrior talked too much of what he had done in battle, his hearers shouted: "See, Iagoo is among us!"

But it was Iagoo who had carved the cradle of Hiawatha long ago, and who had taught him how to make his bow and arrows. And as he sat at the feast, old and ugly but very eager to tell of his adventures, Nokomis said to him: "Good Iagoo, tell us some wonderful story, so that our feast may be more merry," and Iagoo answered like a flash: "You shall hear the most wonderful story that has ever been heard since men have lived upon the earth. You shall hear the strange and marvelous tale of Osseo and his father, King of the Evening Star."

XII

THE SON OF THE EVENING STAR

"SEE the Star of Evening!" cried Iagoo; "see how it shines like a bead of wampum on the robes of the Great Spirit! Gaze on it, and listen to the story of Osseo!

"Long ago, in the days when the heavens were nearer to the earth than they are now, and when the spirits and gods were better known to all men, there lived a hunter in the Northland who had ten daughters, young and beautiful, and as tall as willow-wands. Oweenee, the youngest of these, was proud and wayward, but even fairer than her sisters. When the brave and wealthy warriors came as suitors, each of the ten sisters had many offers, and all except Oweenee were quickly married; but Oweenee laughed at her handsome lovers and sent them all away. Then she married poor, ugly old Osseo, who was bowed down with age, weak with coughing, and twisted and wrinkled like the roots of an oak-tree. For she saw that the spirit of Osseo was far more beautiful than were the painted figures of her handsome lovers.

"All the suitors whom she had refused to marry, and they were many, came and pointed at her with jeers and laughter, and made fun of her and of her husband; but she said to them: 'I care not for your feathers and your wampum; I am happy with Osseo.'

"It happened that the sisters were all invited to a great feast, and they were walking together through the forest, followed by old Osseo and the fair Oweenee; but while all the others chatted gayly, these two walked in silence. Osseo often stopped to gaze at the Star of Evening, and at last the others heard him murmur: 'Oh, pity me, pity me, my Father!' 'He is praying to his father,' said the eldest sister. 'What a shame that the old man does not stumble in the path and break his neck!' and the others all laughed so heartily at the wicked joke that the forest rang with merriment.

"On their way through the thicket, lay a hollow oak that had been uprooted by a storm, and when Osseo saw it he gave a cry of anguish, and leaped into the mighty tree. He went in an old man, ugly and bent and hideous with wrinkles. He came out a splendid youth, straight as an arrow, handsome and very strong. But Osseo was not happy in the change that had come over him. Indeed, he was more sorrowful than ever before, because at the same instant that he recovered his lost youth, Oweenee was changed into a tottering old woman, wasted and worn and ugly as a witch. And her nine hard-hearted sisters and their husbands laughed long and loud, until the forest echoed once again with their wicked merriment.

"Osseo, however, did not turn from Oweenee in her trouble, but took her brown and withered hand, called her sweetheart and soothed her with kind words, until they came to the lodge in the forest where the feast was being given. They sat down to the feast, and all were joyous except Osseo, who would taste neither food nor drink, but sat as if in a dream, looking first at the changed Oweenee, then upward at the sky. All at once he heard a voice come out of the empty air and say to him: 'Osseo, my son, the spells that bound you are now broken, and the evil charms that made you old and withered before your time have all been wished away. Taste the food before you, for it is blessed and will change you to a spirit. Your bowls and your kettles shall be changed to silver and to wampum, and shine like scarlet shells and gleam like the firelight; and all the men and women but Oweenee shall be changed to birds.'

"The voice Osseo heard was taken by the others for the voice of the whippoorwill, singing far off in the lonely forest, and they did not hear a word of what was said. But a sudden tremor ran through the lodge where they sat feasting, and they felt it rise in the air high up above the tree-tops into the starlight. The wooden dishes were changed into scarlet shells, the earthen kettles were changed into silver bowls, and the bark of the roof glittered like the backs of gorgeous beetles.

"Then Osseo saw that the nine beautiful sisters of Oweenee and their husbands, were changed into all sorts of different birds. There were jays and thrushes and magpies and blackbirds, and they flew about the lodge and sang and twittered in many different keys. Only Oweenee was not changed, but remained as wrinkled and old and ugly as before; and Osseo, in his disappointment, gave a cry of anguish such as he had uttered by the oak tree when lo and behold! all Oweenee's former youth and loveliness returned to her. The old woman's staff on which she had been leaning became a glittering silver feather, and her tattered dress was changed into a snowy robe of softest ermine.

"The wigwam trembled once again and floated through the sky until at last it alighted on the Evening Star as gently as thistledown drops to the water, and the ruler of the Evening Star, the father of Osseo, came forward to greet his son.

"'My son,' he said, 'hang the cage of birds that you bring with you at the doorway of my wigwam, and then do you and Oweenee enter,' and Osseo and Oweenee did as they were told, entered the wigwam and listened to the words of Osseo's father.

"'I have had pity on you, my Osseo,' he began. 'I have given back to you your youth and beauty; and I have changed into birds the sisters of Oweenee and their husbands, because they laughed at you and could not see that your spirit was beautiful. When you were an ugly old man, only Oweenee knew your heart. But you must take heed, for in the little star that you see yonder lives an evil spirit, the Wabeno; and it is he who has brought all this sorrow upon you. Take care that you never stand in the light of that evil star. Its gleams are used by the Wabeno as his arrows, and he sits there hating all the world and darting forth his poisonous beams of baleful light to injure all who stray within his reach.'

"For many years Osseo and his father and Oweenee lived happily together upon the Evening Star. Oweenee bore a son to Osseo, and the boy had beauty and courage. Osseo, to please his son, made little bows and arrows for him, and when the boy had learned to shoot, Osseo opened the door of the silver bird-cage and let out all the birds. They darted through the air, singing for joy at their freedom, until the boy bent his bow and struck one of them with a fatal arrow, so that the bird fell wounded at his feet. But when it touched the ground the bird underwent a great change; and there lay at the boy's feet a beautiful young woman with the arrow in her breast.

"As soon as her blood dripped upon the sacred Evening Star, all the magical charms that Osseo's father had used to keep his son and Oweenee with him in the happy dwelling far above the earth were broken, and the boy hunter with his bow and arrow felt himself held by unseen hands, but sinking downward through the blue sky and the empty air until he rested on a green and grassy island in the Big-Sea-Water. Falling and fluttering after him came all the bright birds; and the lodge, with Osseo and Oweenee in it, sailed lightly downward and landed on the island.

"When the bright birds touched the earth, another change came over them, and they became men and women once again as they were before; only they remained so small in size—so tiny, that they were called the Little People, the Puk-Wudjies. And on summer nights, when the stars shone brightly above them, they would dance hand in hand about the island, and sometimes in the starlight they dance there even now."

When the story was finished, Iagoo looked about him at the assembled guests, and added very solemnly: "There are many great men at whom their own people often scoff and jeer. Let these people take warning from the story of Osseo, so that they too may not be changed to birds for laughing at their betters;" and the wedding guests all whispered to each other, "I wonder if he means himself and us." Then Chibiabos sang another sweet and tender love-song, and the guests all went away, leaving Hiawatha alone and happy with Minnehaha.

XIII

BLESSING THE CORNFIELDS

MANY were the pleasant days that followed the wedding of Minnehaha and Hiawatha. All the tribes were at peace with one another, and the hunters roved wherever they chose, built their birch canoes, hunted and fished and trapped the beaver without once hearing the war-cry or the hiss of a hostile arrow. The women made sugar from the sap of the maple-trees, gathered the wild rice and dressed the skins of the deer and beaver, while all around the peaceful village waved green and sunny fields of corn.

Once, when the corn was being planted by the women, the wise and thoughtful Hiawatha said to Minnehaha: "To-night you shall bless the cornfields, and draw around them a magic circle to keep out the mildew and the insects. In the night, when everybody is asleep and none can hear you or see you, rise from your bed, lay aside your clothes and walk in the darkness around the fields of corn that you have planted. Do this and the fields shall be more fruitful and the magic circle of your footsteps cannot be crossed by either worm or insect; for the dragon-fly and the spider, and the grasshopper and the caterpillar all will know that you have walked around the cornfields, and they will not dare to enter."

While Hiawatha spoke, Kahgahgee, King of the Ravens, sat with his band of black robbers in the tree-tops near at hand, and they laughed so loud at the words of Hiawatha that the tree-tops shook and rattled. "Kaw!" shouted the ravens. "Listen to the wise man! Hear the plots of Hiawatha! We will fly over the magic circle and eat just as much corn as we can hold."

When night had fallen dark and black over the fields and woodlands, and when all the Indians were sleeping fast, Minnehaha rose from her bed of branches, laid aside her garments and walked safely among the cornfields, drawing the magic circle of her light footsteps closely around them. No one but the midnight saw her, and no one but the whippoorwill heard the panting of her bosom, for the darkness wrapped its cloak closely about her as she walked. And the dragon-fly and the grasshopper, the spider and the caterpillar, all knew that they could not cross the magic circle of Minnehaha's footsteps.

When the morning came, however, Kahgahgee gathered about him all his black and rascally crew of ravens and jays and crows and blackbirds, shrieking with laughter, and with harsh cries and raucous clamor they all left the tree-tops and flapped eagerly down upon the cornfields. "Kaw! Kaw!" they shrieked, "we will dig up the corn from the soft earth, and we will eat all we can hold, in spite of Minnehaha and her foolish circle!"

But Hiawatha had overheard the ravens as they laughed at him from among the tree-tops. He had risen before day-*break and had covered the cornfields with snares, and at that moment he was hiding in the woods until all the evil birds should alight on the fields and begin their wicked feast.

They came with a rush of wings and hungry cries, settled down upon the cornfields and began to dig and delve and scratch in the earth for the corn that had been planted there, and with all their skill and cunning, they did not see that anything was amiss until their claws were caught in Hiawatha's snares and they were helpless.

Then Hiawatha left his hiding-place among the bushes and strode toward the captive ravens, and his appearance was so awful that the bravest of them hopped and shrieked and flapped their wings in terror. He walked among them, and killed them to the right and left in tens and twenties without mercy; and he hung their dead bodies on poles, to serve as scarecrows and to frighten away all other thieves and robbers from the sacred fields of corn. Only one of the ravens was spared by Hiawatha and that was Kahgahgee, the ruler of them all. Hiawatha tied him with a string and fastened him to the ridge-pole of his wigwam, saying: "Kahgahgee, you are the cause of all this mischief, and I am going to hold you as a warning to all the ravens left alive. If they light upon the cornfields and begin again their wicked thieving, I will kill you and hang your body on a pole as an example." And Hiawatha left Kahgahgee tied fast to the ridge-pole of the wigwam, hopping and tugging angrily at his string and croaking in vain for his friends to come and set him free.

The summer passed, and all the air became warm and soft with the haze of early autumn. The corn had grown tall and yellow, and the ears were almost bursting from their sheaths, when old Nokomis said to Minnehaha: "Let us gather the harvest and strip the ripe ears of all their husks and tassels," and Minnehaha and Nokomis went through the village, calling on the women and the maidens and the young men to come forth and help them with the husking of the corn. All together they went to the cornfields, and the old men and the warriors sat in the shade at the edges of the forest and smoked and looked on in approval, while the young men and maidens stripped the ears of corn and laughed and sang merrily over their labor. Whenever a youth or a maiden found a crooked ear, they all laughed even louder, and crept about the cornfields like weak old men bent almost double with age. But when some lucky maiden found a blood-red ear in the husking, they all cried out: "Ah, Nushka! You shall have a sweetheart!" And the old men nodded in approval as they smoked beneath the pine-trees.

XIV

PICTURE-WRITING

IN those days, the Indians had no way of writing down what they thought, and could only tell each other their messages and their dreams and wisdom, by spoken words. The deeds of hunters and the thoughts of wise men were remembered for a little while, but soon were talked about less often, and when the old men died there were none left who could tell about what had happened in the past. The grave-posts had no marks on them, nor were the Indians able to tell who were buried in the graves. All they knew was that some one of their own tribe, some former wise man or hunter, or some beautiful maiden of other days lay buried there. And Hiawatha was much troubled that the Indians did not know the graves of their own fathers, and could not tell the men who should come after them about the wonderful things that had taken place long before they were born.

Hiawatha spent many days alone in the deep forest, trying to invent some way by which the Indians could always know what had happened in the past, and thereby tell secrets to each other and send messages without the risk of having them forgotten by the messenger. And after a great deal of thought, Hiawatha discovered one of the finest things in all the wide world—a secret that has changed the lives of all Indians since his time.

He took his different colored paints, and began to draw strange figures on the bark of the birch-tree, and every figure had some meaning that the red men would always remember. For the great Manito, God of all the Indians, Hiawatha painted the picture of an egg with different colored points toward the north and the south, the east and the west, to show that the Great Spirit was watching over all the world, and could be found everywhere at once.

For the Evil Spirit, Hiawatha painted the picture of a great serpent to show that the Evil Spirit was as deadly and wicked and treacherous as any snake that crawled in the green marsh grass. For Life and Death, Hiawatha drew two round spots, and painted one of them white and the other black. The white one was meant for Life, because white is clear and fair to look upon; the black was meant for Death, because black is hideous and dark. And Hiawatha painted the sun and the moon and all the stars of heaven, and he painted forests and mountains, lakes and rivers, animals and birds. For the earth he drew a straight line, like the line of the horizon, and for the sky he drew a curved line like a bow. He filled in the space between with white paint that was to mean the white light of day; he painted a point at each side, one for sunrise and the other for sunset, and he drew a number of little stars to represent the night. And Hiawatha drew all sorts of pictures of men and wigwams and bows and arrows and canoes, each with its own meaning, until he had drawn different figures for the different thoughts of men.

He called the Indians to come and see what he had painted, and he said to them: "Look and learn the meaning of these different figures; go and paint upon the graves of those whom you remember, some mark that will always show who it is that lies there buried;" and the Indians painted on the grave-posts of the graves they had not yet forgotten, figures of bear and reindeer, and turtles, and cranes, and beavers. Each one of them invented some sign by which he might always know his dead, and from these signs many of the Indians have been remembered to this day. On their birch canoes the Indians drew many different shapes, and the brightest of them all was the figure of Love. It was painted in deep scarlet, because scarlet is the strongest of all colors, and the color meant: "I am greater than all others;" for the Indians believed that love was mightier than life or death, and more dangerous than either war or hunting.

Other figures were also painted there, and by looking at the pictures drawn by an Indian you could tell who he was, and what family he came from, and whether he was stern and cruel or loving and kind-hearted. For the Indians were apt to paint the things they thought about the most.

Many were the gifts that Hiawatha gave his people; but when he taught them how to paint their thoughts, he gave them a better gift than any other.

XV

HIAWATHA'S LAMENTATION

WHEN Hiawatha lived, there were many evil spirits on the earth; and these evil spirits were very jealous of the friendship between Hiawatha and Chibiabos. "If we can only get this Chibiabos in our power," they plotted, "we will kill him, and when he is dead, Hiawatha cannot do so much good to all the tribes of men; for Chibiabos helps him like a brother, and together they are much too strong for us." The evil spirits joined to destroy both Chibiabos and Hiawatha, and they laid many traps and thought of many schemes to catch the two friends off their guard.

Hiawatha was so wise that he knew of all this plotting, and he often said to Chibiabos: "O my brother, stay with me always, for together the evil spirits cannot do us any harm." But Chibiabos was young and heedless and he did not fear the evil spirits. He laughed at Hiawatha, and said to him: "Harm and evil never come near me, my Hiawatha; have no fear on my account." But Hiawatha only shook his head, and feared all the more because Chibiabos feared so little.

Once in the winter time, when the Big-Sea-Water was covered with ice and snow, Chibiabos was hunting a buck with antlers, and the buck ran right across the frozen lake. Wild with excitement of hunting, Chibiabos followed him and ran far out from shore upon the treacherous ice, where the evil spirits were waiting for him. When they saw that he was far enough from land, they broke the ice and Chibiabos fell with a crash and a splash into the freezing water of the lake. Even then he might have saved himself and climbed out upon the ice but the strong, cruel water-god, the god of the Dacotahs, wrapped his cold wet arms around the body of Chibiabos and dragged him down, down through the dark black water to the bottom. There the water-god buried him beneath the mud and sand, so that his dead body might not rise to the surface; and the evil spirits danced for joy at the death of Chibiabos. "We have killed him," they shouted gleefully to one another; "we have killed the sweetest singer in the world and the dearest friend of Hiawatha!"

From the headlands on the shore, Hiawatha had seen Chibiabos plunge into the lake, and he heard the wicked shouting of the evil spirits. He gave such a cry of sorrow that the forest trembled, and the wolves on the prairie raised their heads to listen and then howled in answer, while the hoarse thunder stirred itself among the mountains and awakened all the echoes to his cry.

Then Hiawatha smeared his face with black paint, the color of sorrow and of death; he covered his head with his robe and sat for seven long weeks in his wigwam, grieving for the murdered Chibiabos. And the fir-trees sadly waved their dark green branches to and fro above his head and sighed as mournfully as Hiawatha.

Spring came, and all the birds and animals, and even the rivulets, and flowers and grasses, looked in vain for the dead Chibiabos. The bluebird sang a song of sorrow from the tree-tops; the robin echoed it from the silence of the thicket, and the whippoorwill took up the sad refrain at night and wailed it far and wide through all the woodland. "Chibiabos! Chibiabos!" murmured every living thing, and all the echoes sighed in answer until the whole world seemed to mourn for the lost singer.

Then the wise men of the tribes—the medicine-men, the men of magic—came to Hiawatha as he sat in sorrow in his hut, and they walked before him in a grave procession to drive the sadness from his heart. Each of them carried a pouch of healing, made of beaver-skin or lynx or otter, and filled with roots and herbs of wonderful power to cure all diseases and to drive the evil spirits of grief from the heart and from the mind. To and fro they walked, until Hiawatha uncovered his head, washed the black paint from his face, and followed the wise men to the Sacred Lodge that they had built beside his own wigwam.

There they gave to Hiawatha a marvelous drink made of spearmint and yarrow and all sorts of strange and different roots, and when he had drunk of this they began a wild and mystic dance, beating on the small drums that they carried, and shaking their pouches of healing in the face of Hiawatha. "Hi-au-ha!" they shouted in strange voices, "*way-ha-way!* We can cure you, Hiawatha; we can make you strong." And they shook their medicine pouches over Hiawatha's head, and continued beating on their hollow drums, as they circled wildly around him again and again.

All at once the sorrow left Hiawatha's heart, as the ice is swept from a river in the springtime, and like a man awakening from evil dreams he felt that he was healed, and he gazed about him where the medicine-men were still dancing. They were trying to summon Chibiabos from his grave deep down in the sandy bottom of the Big-Sea-Water, for the water-god had buried him so deep that his spirit could not go into the land of dead men, but was still in his drowned body, struggling to free itself. And the magic of the wise men was so strong that Chibiabos rose body and all, and stood on the bottom of the lake, listening to them.

Then the dead man floated to the shore, climbed out upon the bank and made his way swiftly and silently through the forest to the doorway of the wigwam where the medicine-men were singing. When he shook the curtain of the doorway and peered in upon them they would not let him enter, but gave him through an opening in the door a burning torch and told him to light a fire in the land of spirits, so that all who died might see it and find their way thither; and they made Chibiabos ruler in the Kingdom of the Dead. He left the doorway of the wigwam and vanished in the forest, and the wise men watched the twinkling of his torch until it disappeared. They saw that the branches did not move as he passed, and that the dead leaves and the grass did not even bend or rustle beneath his footsteps, and they looked at one another much afraid, because such sights are not good for living men to see.

Four days Chibiabos traveled down the pathway of the dead, and for his food he ate the dead man's strawberry. He saw many other dead men struggling under heavy burdens of food and skins and wampum that their friends had given them to use in the Land of Spirits, and they groaned beneath their burdens. He passed them all, crossed the sad, dark River of Death upon the swinging log that floats there; and at last he came to the Lake of Silver, and was carried in the Stone Canoe over the water to the Islands of the Blessed, where he rules all ghosts and shadows.

When he had disappeared in the dark forest, Hiawatha left the Sacred Lodge and wandered eastward and westward teaching men the use of roots and herbs and the cure of all disorders; and thus was first made known to the Indians the sacred knowledge of caring for the sick.

XVI

PAU-PUK-KEEWIS

YOU remember how Pau-Puk-Keewis danced the Beggar's Dance at Hiawatha's wedding, and how, in his wild leaping and whirling at the edges of the Big-Sea-Water, he tossed up the mighty sand dunes of the Nagow Wudjoo. And you remember also, how the warriors all disliked Pau-Puk-Keewis, and called him an idler and coward, for they knew his heart was bad within him. Only the women cared for Pau-Puk-Keewis, and the women were deceived by his handsome face and his costly dresses.

One morning Pau-Puk-Keewis came in search of adventures to the village, and found all the young men gathered in the wigwam of Iagoo, listening to the wonderful stories that old Iagoo always told when any one would hear him. He was telling how Ojeeg, the Summer-Maker, climbed up to the sky and made a hole in Heaven that let out all the warm and pleasant weather of the summer months. He was describing how the Otter tried it first, and how the Beaver and the Lynx and Badger also tried it, all of them climbing to the top of the highest mountain and hitting their heads against the sky.

"They cracked it but they could not break it," said Iagoo, "and then Ojeeg the Weasel came and the Wolverine helped him to make ready for the trial. Ojeeg climbed to the top of the mountain, and the Wolverine went with him. The Wolverine crouched down like a grasshopper on the mountain top, with his legs all drawn up beneath him like a squirrel or a cricket, and he leaped as hard as he was able at the sky.

"The first time he leaped," said Iagoo, "the sky bent above him as the ice in rivers when the water rises beneath it in the springtime. The second time he leaped, the sky cracked open, and he could see the light of Heaven shining through. And the third time he leaped—crash! The sky broke into bits above him and he disappeared in Heaven, followed closely by the valiant Weasel, who tumbled into Heaven after him and has been called 'The Summer-Maker' ever since."

"Hark you," cried Pau-Puk-Keewis, bursting through the open doorway of the wigwam. "I am tired of all this talk, and I am tired of Hiawatha's endless wisdom. Listen to me, and you shall learn something more interesting than old Iagoo's stories. Watch, and I will teach you all a splendid game."

From his pouch he drew forth all the pieces used in the game of Bowl and Counters. There were thirteen in all, and nine were painted white on one side and red on the other; while four were made of brass, one side polished and the other painted black. On nine of the thirteen pieces were painted pictures of men, or ducks, or serpents, and Pau-Puk-Keewis shook them all together in a wooden bowl and tossed them out, explaining that the score was counted great or little according to the way the pictures and the colors fell upon the ground. Curious eyes stared at him as he shook and tossed and counted up the pieces, until the Indians were drawn into the game one after one, and they sat there playing for prizes of weapons and fur robes and wampum through the rest of the day and through the night until the sun rose once again. By that time the clever, lucky Pau-Puk-Keewis had won everything they owned—deerskin shirts, wampum, pipes, ermine robes and all sorts of weapons, and he chuckled to himself.

Then the crafty Pau-Puk-Keewis said to them: "My wigwam is lonely, and I want a companion in my wanderings. I want a slave. I will risk all the wampum and the fur robes, everything that I have won, against the nephew of Iagoo—that young man who is standing yonder. But if I win again, he shall be my slave for life."

"Done!" cried Iagoo, his eyes glowing like coals beneath his shaggy brows, and he seized the bowl and shook it fiercely, throwing out the pieces on the ground. Pau-Puk-Keewis counted, took the bowl and threw in his turn, and his throw was far more lucky than that of old Iagoo. "The game is mine!" cried Pau-Puk-Keewis, smiling as he rose and looked about him, and heaped all the robes and feathers and wampum and weapons in the arms of Iagoo's nephew, now a slave.

"Carry them to my wigwam yonder," said Pau-Puk-Keewis, "and wait there until I have need of you;" and he left the tent, followed by the angry glances of all the other players, who had lost all their fine furs and wampum belts and even the pipes they had been smoking.

Pau-Puk-Keewis strolled through the sunny morning singing to himself, for his new wealth made him very happy, and he soon reached the farthest wigwam of the village, which was the home of Hiawatha.

Nobody was there. Only Kahgahgee, the raven, tied to the ridge-pole, screamed and flapped his wings, watching Pau-Puk-Keewis with glaring eyes.

"All are gone," said Pau-Puk-Keewis, thinking of new mischief as he spoke; "all are gone, and they have left the lodge for me to do with as I choose."

He seized the raven by the neck and whirled him around in the air like a rattle, until the bird was strangled, and he left Kahgahgee's dead body dangling from the ridge-pole as an insult to Hiawatha. Then he went inside and threw everything into the wildest disorder, piling together all the kettles and bowls, and all the skins and buffalo-robes that he could find as an insult to Minnehaha and to Nokomis; and he ran off through the forest, whistling and singing, much pleased with what he had done.

He climbed the rocks that overlooked the Big-Sea-Water, and rested lazily upon his back, gazing up into the sky and listening to the splash of the waves on the beaches far beneath. The sea-gulls fluttered about him in great flocks, very curious to know what he was doing, and before they could get out of his way he had killed them by tens and twenties and had thrown the dead bodies over the cliff down to the beaches. One of the sea-gulls, who was perched on a crag above, shouted out: "It is Pau-Puk-Keewis, and he is killing us by the hundred. Fly quickly and send a message to our brother! Hasten and bring the news to Hiawatha!"

XVII

THE HUNTING OF PAU-PUK-KEEWIS

WHEN Hiawatha heard of the mischief that Pau-Puk-Keewis had worked among the gulls he was very angry indeed; but when he discovered the wrecked wigwam and the dead body of the raven, and heard how Pau-Puk-Keewis had despoiled Iagoo and his friends of their robes and pipes and wampum, he swore that he would kill Pau-Puk-Keewis with his own hand.

"The world is not so wide but I will find him!" cried out Hiawatha; "the way is not so rough but I will reach him with my anger!" and with several hunters Hiawatha set out upon the trail of Pau-Puk-Keewis.

They followed it to the crags where he had killed the gulls, but by that time Pau-Puk-Keewis was far away among the lowlands, and turning back he saw his pursuers on the mountain and waved his arms to mock them.

Hiawatha shouted at him from the mountain top: "The world is not so rough and wide but I shall catch you, Pau-Puk-Keewis. Hide where you will, but I shall find you out," and Pau-Puk-Keewis sped forward like an antelope for Hiawatha's words had made him suddenly afraid.

He rushed through the forest until he came to a little stream that had overflowed its banks, and there he saw a dam made by the beavers. Pau-Puk-Keewis stood on the dam and called, and the King of Beavers, Ahmeek, rose to the surface of the water to find out who the stranger might be.

"Ahmeek, my friend," said Pau-Puk-Keewis, "the water is very cool and pleasant. Let me dive in and stay with you awhile! Change me into a beaver like yourself, so that I may rest with you in your lodge beneath the water."

"Wait awhile," said Ahmeek, looking at him cautiously. "I must ask the other beavers," and he sank beneath the water like a stone.

Pau-Puk-Keewis thought he could hear Hiawatha and the hunters crashing through the forest, and he waded out upon the dam, calling to the beavers until one head after another popped up out of the water, and all the beavers in the pond were looking at him.

"Your dwelling is very pleasant, my friends," said Pau-Puk-Keewis in an entreating voice; "cannot you change me also into a beaver?"

"Yes," said Ahmeek, "let yourself slide down into the water and you shall become as we are."

Pau-Puk-Keewis slid down into the water and his deer-skin shirt and moccasins and leggings became black and shiny. His fringes drew together into a clump, and became a broad black tail; his teeth became sharp, and long whiskers sprouted out from his cheeks. He was changed into a beaver.

"Make me large," he said, as he swam about the pond; "make me ten times larger than the other beavers," and Ahmeek said: "Yes, when you enter our lodge beneath the water you shall be ten times as large as any one of us."

They sank down through the water, and Pau-Puk-Keewis saw great stores of food upon the bottom. They entered the lodge and came up inside of it above the surface of the water, and the lodge was divided into large rooms, with ledges on which the beavers slept. There they made Pau-Puk-Keewis ten times larger than any other beaver, and they said to him: "Thenceforth you shall rule over all the rest of us and be our king."

But Pau-Puk-Keewis had not been sitting long upon the throne of the beavers, when he heard the voice of the beaver watchman call out from among the water-lilies: "Hiawatha, Hiawatha!" There was a shout and a noise of rending branches, and the water sucked out of the beavers' lodge and left it high and dry; their dam was broken. The hunters jumped on the roof of the lodge and broke a great hole in it, through which the sunlight streamed as the beavers scuttled away through their doorway to seek safety in deeper water. But Pau-Puk-Keewis was so big, and so puffed up with heavy feeding and the pride of being a king, that he could not crawl through the doorway with the others, but was helpless before the hunters.

Hiawatha looked through the roof and cried: "Ah, Pau-Puk-Keewis, I know you in spite of your disguise. I said that you could not escape me," and Hiawatha and his hunters beat Pau-Puk-Keewis with their heavy clubs until the beaver's skull was broken into pieces.

Six tall hunters bore the body of the beaver homeward, and it was so heavy that they had to carry it slung from poles and branches that rested on their shoulders. But within the dead body Pau-Puk-Keewis still lived, and thought and felt exactly as a man; and at last, with great effort he gathered himself together, left the beaver's body and, assuming once more his own form, he vanished in the forest.

Hiawatha saw the figure as it stole away amid the shadows of the pine-trees, and with a shout he leaped to his feet and gave chase with all his hunters, who followed the flying Pau-Puk-Keewis as the rain follows the wind. The hunted man, all breathless and worn out, came to a large lake in the middle of the forest, and there he saw the wild geese that we call the brant, swimming and diving among the water-lilies and enjoying themselves upon the water.

"O my brothers," called Pau-Puk-Keewis, "change me to a brant with shining feathers and two strong wings to carry me wherever I will go, and make me ten times larger than any of you!"

At once they changed him into a huge brant, ten times larger than the others, and with loud cries and a clamor of wings they rose in the air and flew high up into the sunlight. As they flew they said to Pau-Puk-Keewis: "Take care that you do not look downward as you fly, or something strange and terrible will happen to you."

But suddenly they heard a sound of shouting far beneath them, and Pau-Puk-Keewis, who recognized the voice of Iagoo and the tones of Hiawatha, forgot the warning about looking downward, and drew in his long black neck to gaze upon the distant village. The swift wind that was blowing behind him caught his mighty tail-feathers, tipped him over, and Pau-Puk-Keewis, struggling in vain to get his balance, fell through the clear air like a heavy stone. He heard the shouting of the people grow louder and louder; he saw the brant become little specks in the air above him, and plunging downward the great goose struck the ground with a heavy, sullen thud and lay there dead.

But Pau-Puk-Keewis still lived in the crushed body of the giant bird, and he swiftly took his own form again and rushed along the shore of the Big-Sea-Water, with Hiawatha close upon his heels. And Hiawatha shouted at him as they ran: "The world is not so rough and wide but I shall catch you, Pau-Puk-Keewis. Hide where you will, but I shall reach you with my anger!" and he was so close to Pau-Puk-Keewis that he shot out his right hand to seize him by the shoulder. Pau-Puk-Keewis spun around in a circle, whirled the dust into the air and leaped into a hollow oak tree, where he changed himself into a serpent and came gliding out among the roots.

Hiawatha broke the tree to pieces with a blow of his magic mittens; but there was no Pau-Puk-Keewis inside of it, and Hiawatha saw him once again in his own form, running like the wind along the beach.

They ran until they came to the painted sand-stone rocks where the Old Man of the Mountain has his home, and the Old Man opened the doorway of the rocks and gave Pau-Puk-Keewis a hiding-place in the gloomy caverns underneath the mountains, shutting the rock doorway with a heavy crash as Hiawatha threw himself upon it. With his magic mittens Hiawatha knocked great holes in the rocks, crying out in tones of thunder: "Open! Open! I am Hiawatha!" But the Old Man of the Mountain did not answer.

Then Hiawatha raised his hands to the heavens and implored the lightning and the thunder to come to his aid and break the rocks of sandstone into fragments, and the lightning and the thunder came snarling and rumbling over the Big-Sea-Water at the call of Hiawatha. Together Hiawatha and the lightning split the rock doorway into fragments, and the thunder boomed among the caverns, shouting: "Where is Pau-Puk-Keewis!"

Pau-Puk-Keewis lay dead among the caves of sandstone, killed by Hiawatha and the lightning and thunder. This time he was dead indeed, crushed by the rocks that had fallen upon him, and killed in his own form so he might never rise again.

Hiawatha took the ghost of Pau-Puk-Keewis and changed it into a great eagle that wheels and circles in the air to this day, screaming from the mountain peaks and gliding in great slants over deep and empty valleys. In winter, when the wind whirled the snow in drifts and eddies around the wigwams, the Indians would say to one another: "There is Pau-Puk-Keewis, come from the mountains to dance once more among the villages," and when we see great hills of sifted snow, heaped high and white by winter wind, we may think of Pau-Puk-Keewis and his dance among the sand dunes.

XVIII

THE DEATH OF KWASIND

THE name and fame of Kwasind, the strong man, had spread among all tribes of Indians, and in all the world there was nobody who dared to wrestle or to strive with this mighty friend of Hiawatha. But the little pigmy people, the mischievous Puk-Wudjies, plotted against Kwasind, for they were very much afraid of him, and thought he would destroy them.

"If this great fellow goes on breaking whatever he touches, tearing things to pieces and filling the whole world with wonder at his deeds, what will happen to us?" cried the Little People; "what will become of the Puk-Wudjies? He will step on us as if we were mushrooms; he will drive us into the water, and give our bodies to the wicked *Nee-ba-naw-baigs* to be eaten." And all the Little People plotted to murder the cruel and wicked, dangerous, heartless Kwasind.

There was one secret about Kwasind that nobody on earth knew, except himself and the clever Little People. All his strength and all his weakness came from the crown of his head. Nowhere but on the crown of his head could any weapon do him harm, and even there nothing would hurt him except the blue seed-cone that grows upon the fir-tree. The Little People had discovered this by their great skill in magic, and they gathered together the blue cones of the fir-tree and piled them in great heaps upon the red rock ledges that overhung the river Taquamenaw. There they sat and waited until Kwasind should pass by in his canoe.

It was a hot summer afternoon when Kwasind, the strong man, in his birch canoe came floating slowly down the Taquamenaw. The air was very still and very warm; the insects buzzed and hummed above the silent water, and the locust sang from the dry, sweet-smelling bushes on the shore.

In Kwasind's ears there was a drowsy murmur, and he felt the spirits of sleep beat upon his forehead with their soft little war-clubs. At the first blow his head nodded with slumber; at the second blow his paddle trailed motionless in the water, and at the third his eyes closed and he went fast asleep, sitting bolt upright in his canoe. The warm air quivered on the water, the midges and the gnats sang in tiny voices, and the locust once more struck up his shrill tune from the river bank, when the sentinels of the Little People went scampering down the beach, calling out shrilly that Kwasind was sound asleep in his canoe and drifting nearer and nearer to the fatal red rocks that overhung the river. And all the Little People climbed the rocks and peered down upon the water, waiting until Kwasind should pass beneath.

At last the canoe swung sideways around a bend in the river and came drifting down the slow-moving current as lightly as an alder-leaf, and the Little People moved the fir-cones nearer to the edge and crouched there waiting.

"Death to Kwasind!" they shouted in little voices as the canoe glided underneath the rocks, "Death to Kwasind!" and they rained down showers of blue fir-cones right on the defenseless head of the sleeping giant.

As a great boulder is tipped into a stream, Kwasind tottered sideways from his canoe, struck the water with a sullen plunge that tossed the spray high in the air, and the waters closed above him with a mighty sob. Bottom upward his canoe drifted down the river, and nothing was seen or heard of Kwasind from that day to this. But his memory lived long among the Indians, who would tell their children of his great feats of strength, and show to them the boulder that Kwasind had pitched into the swift Pauwating River when he was little more than a boy.

When the gales of winter tossed the pine-trees and roared among the branches until they groaned and split with a terrible noise of rending wood, the Indians would say to one another, as they sat in their warm wigwams and listened to the wind shake the forest to its roots: "There goes Kwasind, gathering his firewood!" and in the country where he lived near the Big-Sea-Water there are still many marks of his great strength that will show, to any who care to see, what a mighty man this Kwasind was.

XIX

THE GHOSTS

THE vulture never drops from the heavens to seize his prey upon the desert but some other vulture views his plunge and follows swiftly.

Other vultures see the second, and in a few minutes their victim finds a row of them before him and the air dark with their wings.

Just so do troubles come upon human beings, not one at a time but together, until the unhappy man or woman finds the air as black as midnight with their shadows, and in this way did troubles pursue the unfortunate Hiawatha. First Chibiabos died—murdered by the evil spirits. Then Kwasind was killed as he drifted down the stream asleep in his canoe; and then in the dark winter, when the ice had bound the rivers and the trees were naked in the bitter air, another sorrow came upon Hiawatha. But before it came he had a strange adventure, and from this he knew that he would be forced to undergo some mighty trial.

One black, wintry evening after the sun had set, Nokomis and Minnehaha were sitting together in their wigwam waiting for Hiawatha to return from the hunt, when they heard light and measured footsteps on the snow, and the curtain that hung in the doorway of their lodge was slowly lifted. Two shadowy figures entered—two women, who seemed strangers in the village; and, without a word, they took their seats in the darkest corner of the wigwam and crouched there silently and sadly, shivering with cold. Their faces were very white, their clothes were thin and torn, and they would not answer anything that Nokomis or Minnehaha said to them.

Was it the wind blowing down the smoke-flue, or was it the hooting of the owl that made both Minnehaha and Nokomis think that they heard a voice come out of the darkness and say to them: "These are dead people that sit before you and share your fire! They are ghosts from the Land of the Hereafter, who have come to haunt you!" At all events they thought that such a voice cried out to them, and they were very much afraid when Hiawatha entered, fresh from hunting, and laid the red deer he had been carrying at the feet of Minnehaha.

Never before did Hiawatha appear so handsome, and Minnehaha thought him even nobler than when he came to woo her by the waterfall in the land of the Dacotahs.

Turning Hiawatha saw the two strange guests who had not said a word when he had entered, but crouched silently in the darkest corner of the wigwam, with their hoods drawn over their white faces. Only their eyes gleamed like dull coals as they gazed upon the firelight. But Hiawatha did not ask a single question, although he wondered greatly, and he set about preparing the deer for their evening meal.

When the meat was ready, the two guests, still without saying a word, sprang like wolves from their corners, seized upon the choicest parts, the white fat that Hiawatha had saved for Minnehaha, and retreated with their portions back to the shadow of their corner. And although Hiawatha and Minnehaha and Nokomis were amazed by the strange actions of their guests, they did not show it by word or look, but acted as if nothing had happened. Only Minnehaha found time to whisper to Hiawatha: "They are famished; let them eat of what they will."

Many days passed, and the two strange women still sat cowering in their corner of the wigwam; but at night, when everybody slept, they went out into the gloomy forest and brought back wood and pine-cones for the fire. Whenever Hiawatha returned from hunting or fishing, and the evening meal had been prepared, they would leap from their dark corner, seize the very choicest portions that had been set aside for Minnehaha, and without any question being asked them, or any blame for their strange conduct, they would flit back into the darkest shadow and devour their food like hungry wolves.

Never once did Nokomis or Minnehaha or Hiawatha reprove them by a single word or look, preferring to endure the insult rather than to break in any way the law of hospitality and the sacred custom of free-giving; and through it all the pale, sad women never said a word.

One night, however, Hiawatha lay awake, watching the embers of the fire, when he heard loud groans and sobbing, and saw the two strange guests sitting bolt upright on their couches, weeping bitterly. And Hiawatha asked them: "O my guests, why is it that you are so unhappy and weep together in the middle of the night? Has old Nokomis or Minnehaha wronged you in any way or failed to treat you with proper courtesy?"

The two women left off weeping, and answered in low and gentle voices: "Hiawatha, we are spirits. We are the souls of those who once lived here on earth, and we have come from the kingdom of Chibiabos to warn you.

"Every cry of sorrow for the dead is heard in the Land of Spirits, and calls back those of us for whom you mourn. We are much saddened by this useless sorrow, and we have come from the Blessed Islands to ask you to tell all your people what we say. Do not vex our ears with weeping, and do not lay upon our graves so many robes, and kettles, and wampum-belts, for the spirits find these a heavy burden. Only give us food to carry with us on our journey, and see that a fire is lighted for us on the four nights following our death. For the journey to the Land of Spirits takes four days and four nights, and the cheerful firelight saves us from groping in the darkness. Now farewell, Hiawatha. We have put you to a great trial and have found you brave and noble. Do not fail in the greater trial and the harder struggle that you will shortly have to suffer."

Their voices died away, and sudden darkness filled the wigwam. Hiawatha heard the rustle of their garments as they passed him, saw a gleam of starlight as they lifted the curtain from the doorway; and when he rekindled the fire he found that the pale, sad women, his strange guests, had disappeared.

XX

THE FAMINE

OH, the cruel and bitter winter that followed! The ice on the rivers and lakes became thicker and harder than ever before; the snow on the fields and in the forests was so deep that the Indians could hardly force their way out of their buried wigwams. No game ran through the frozen thickets, no birds flew among the trees. In the level snow the starving hunters could not find a single track of deer or rabbit, and the corn in the village became less and less until it was all gone. Then the children began to cry with hunger, the women went about with faces pinched and drawn, and the men drew their belts tighter day by day. At night the stars in the heavens seemed to glare like the eyes of famished wolves, and the cold wind moaned among the trees as if the very air were suffering from want. It was an evil time.

When the famine was at its worst, two more strange guests came to the wigwam of Hiawatha; nor did they linger at the doorway and wait to be invited in. They entered without a word, and with sunken eyes they gazed at Minnehaha, and one of them said in a hollow voice: "Look on me! My name is Famine," and the other one cried out: "I am Fever!"

The lovely Minnehaha shivered when she saw them, and a great chill came over her. She lay down on her bed and hid her face, and as the wicked guests continued to gaze she felt first burning heat, then icy coldness dart like arrows through her body. Hiawatha rushed into the forest to find some food for Minnehaha and to drive away the awful visitors; but the forest was bleak and empty, and there was no food to be had. "Ah Great Manito!" cried out Hiawatha, "give me food for my dying Minnehaha, before the Fever and Famine tear her from me forever!" But the Great Manito did not answer, and the silent forest only murmured dully, echoing the words of Hiawatha. With his bow and arrows he strode for miles through the deserted woods where he had once led his young bride homeward from the land of the Dacotahs. But now no animals peeped at him from amid the tree trunks, and there was no cheerful fluttering and singing from the branches; everything was deathly silent, muffled in a mighty cloak of snow.

"SEVEN LONG DAYS AND NIGHTS HE SAT THERE"—
Page 293

While he was searching in vain for food, the two dark figures in the wigwam drew closer and closer to Minnehaha, until they crouched at either side of her bed of branches, and one of them said in hollow tones: "My name is Famine," and the other cried out: "I am Fever!" and they leaned over the bed and fixed their sunken eyes on Minnehaha, and Nokomis could not frighten them away.

"Hark!" said Minnehaha as the Fever gazed upon her, "I hear a rushing and a roaring. I hear the falls of Minnehaha calling to me from the land of the Dacotahs!"

"No, my child," said Nokomis, "it is nothing but the wind of night that blows amid the pine trees."

"Look!" said Minnehaha, as the Fever drew still closer to her bed. "I see my father standing in his doorway. I see him beckoning to me from his wigwam!"

"Ah no, my child," said Nokomis sadly; "it is nothing but the smoke of our fire curling upward to the smoke-flue."

"Oh," said Minnehaha, "I see the eyes of Death glaring at me in the darkness! I feel his icy fingers clasping mine! Hiawatha! Hiawatha!"

24

The wretched Hiawatha, miles away in the dark forest, heard Minnehaha cry to him and he hurried homeward with a sinking heart, but before he reached his wigwam he heard the voice of Nokomis wailing through the night. What a sight met his eyes as he burst into his dreary lodge! Nokomis was rocking sadly to and fro, moaning and weeping; and Minnehaha lay, cold and dead, upon her bed of branches!

Hiawatha gave such a cry of sorrow that the forest shuddered and groaned, and even the stars in heaven trembled. Then he sat down at the feet of Minnehaha, and covered his face with both his hands. Seven days and nights he sat there without moving or speaking, and he did not know whether it was night or day.

At last he rose and wrapped Minnehaha in her softest robes of ermine, and they made a grave for her in the snow beneath the hemlock trees. Four nights they kindled a fire on her grave, so that her soul might have cheerful light upon its journey to the Blessed Islands, and Hiawatha watched from the doorway of his wigwam to see that the fire was burning brightly so she might never be left in darkness, and he said: "Farewell, my Minnehaha! My heart is buried with you, and before long my task here will be finished and I will join you in the Blessed Islands. Soon I shall follow in your footsteps to the Land of Hereafter!"

XXI

THE WHITE MAN'S FOOT

IN a lodge built close beside a frozen river sat an old man, whose hair was whiter than the whitest snow, and he shook and trembled as he sat there, hearing nothing but the gale that raged outside and seeing nothing but the flakes of snow that leaped and whirled about his chilly wigwam. All the coals of his fire were covered with white ashes and the fire itself was dying away unheeded, when a bright youth with red blood in his cheeks walked lightly through the open doorway. On his head was a crown of fresh and sweet-smelling grasses; his lips were curved in a beautiful smile, and he carried in his hand a bunch of flowers that filled the lodge with the fragrance of the wildwood.

"Ah, my son," said the old man, "it does my old eyes good to gaze upon you! Take a seat beside my fire, and we will pass the night together! Tell me of your travels and your strange adventures, and let me tell you of all the wonderful deeds that I have done."

The old man drew a peace-pipe from his pouch, filled it with willow-bark and handed it to the beautiful young stranger, who smoked in silence while he listened to the old man's words.

"When I blow my breath about me," said the old man, "the water becomes as hard as stone and the rivers cannot move."

"When I breathe upon the meadows and the woodlands," answered the young stranger with a sunny smile, "the flowers rise like magic, and the rivers, with a song, go rushing on again."

"When I shake my long white hair," said the old man scowling, "the land is buried with snow and the leaves all fade away and fall to earth. When I raise my voice the ground becomes like flint, the wild fowl fly away and the wild beasts of the forest hide for fear."

"When I shake my flowing ringlets," said the young man with a light laugh, "the warm rain falls on the hills and fields, and the wild geese and the heron come back to the marshes. Homeward flies the swallow, and the robin and the bluebird sing for joy. Wherever I go the woodlands ring with music, and the meadows become blue with violets."

While they were speaking, the great sun leaped up above the horizon and shot his beams of orange gold through the doorway of the wigwam. The air became warm and pleasant, and in the light of morning the young stranger saw the icy face of the old man and knew that he had spent the night with Peboan, the winter. From the old man's eyes the tears were running in two streams, the water was dripping from his hair, and his body shrank until it vanished into the ground. And on the hearth-stone where the old man's fire had been smoking, blossomed the earliest flower of springtime.

Thus did the young stranger, Spring, come back again and drive away the icy chill of that dreadful winter of famine and death. To the northward passed the wild swans, calling to one another, and the bluebirds and the pigeons and the robins sang in the thicket, until the grieving Hiawatha heard their voices and went forth from his gloomy wigwam to gaze up into the warm, blue sky.

From his wanderings in the east returned Iagoo, the great boaster, full of stories more wonderful than any that he had ever told, and the people laughed as they listened to him, saying: "Cold and famine have not harmed Iagoo; he is just the same as ever, and has seen more wonders in his travels than the Great Manito himself."

"I have seen a water greater than the Big-Sea-Water," cried Iagoo, "much greater! And over it came a huge canoe, with large white wings that carried it along!"

"It can't be true!" cried all the Indians, laughing at Iagoo; "we don't believe one word of what you say."

"From the canoe," went on Iagoo, "came thunder and lightning, and a hundred warriors landed on the beach. Their faces were painted white, and there was hair upon their chins."

"What lies you tell us!" shouted all the people. "Do not think that we believe you!" Hiawatha only did not join in the roar of laughter that Iagoo's words called forth from all the men and women and children who were listening.

"What he tells is true," said Hiawatha, "I have seen it all in a dream. I have seen the great canoe of the white-faced people come sailing from the Land of Sunrise. I have seen these people moving swiftly westward under the guidance of the Great Manito, until the fires of their wigwams smoked in all the valleys, while their canoes rushed over all the lakes and rivers. Let us welcome them," said Hiawatha; "let us give them of our best and call them brothers, for the Great Manito has sent them and they come to do his bidding.

25

"Then I had another vision," Hiawatha went on sadly. "I saw our people fighting with one another, forgetful of the warning of the Great Manito. And the forests where we hunted, and the rivers where we fished and trapped the beaver, knew our faces and our voices no more; for our people were scattered like the autumn leaves, until no Indians were left upon the earth." And when his voice died away, the Indians all sat in silence and looked at one another with a sudden fear.

XXII

HIAWATHA'S DEPARTURE

ON the shore of the Big-Sea-Water, in the sunny morning, Hiawatha stood in the doorway of his wigwam, gazing out over the shining lake. The sky was bright and blue above him, the pebbles sparkled on the beaches, and the still water reflected the great pine-trees of the forest. Every trace of sorrow was gone from Hiawatha's face, and with a smile of joy he lifted his open hands toward the blazing sun to shade his eyes. He was watching something that floated far out on the water—some image which he could not plainly see, but which was drawing nearer and nearer to the village. At last he saw that it was a birch canoe, with paddles flashing as they rose and fell; and in it came the white-faced people from the Land of Sunrise, led by a bearded chief in a black robe, who wore a cross upon his breast.

The canoe grated on the pebbles, and Hiawatha, with his hands stretched outward as a sign of friendship, called to them in welcome.

"The sun is fair to look upon, O strangers," cried out Hiawatha. "Our town waits for you in peace, and the doors of all our wigwams stand open to receive you. Our tobacco never was so sweet and pleasant, and our waving cornfields never seemed so beautiful to behold as this morning, when you visit us from far-off lands." And the chief of the strange people, the bearded man in the black robe, answered, stammering a little, for the language of the Indians was strange to him: "May the peace of Christ be with you and your people, Hiawatha!"

Then the noble-hearted Hiawatha led them to his wigwam, where he seated them on skins of bison and ermine, while Nokomis brought them water in cups of birch-bark and food in bowls of polished basswood; and when they were done with eating, peace-pipes were filled with willow-bark and lighted for them to smoke.

All the warriors, and old men, and the magicians of the village came to welcome the great strangers, and they sat around the doorway of Hiawatha's wigwam in a large circle, smoking their pipes and waiting for the strangers to come forth and to speak to them. The black-robed chief went out of the wigwam and greeted all the Indians, while they said to him: "O Brother, it is well that you have come so far to see us!"

Then the bearded man in the black robe commenced to speak, showing them the cross that he wore upon his breast, and he told them about Christ and the Virgin Mary and how the wicked tribe, the Jews, had taken Christ and crucified him long ago, and the Indians smoked on in silence, listening to his words.

"It is well," they said when he had finished; "we will think upon your words of wisdom. We are pleased."

Then they rose and went home to their wigwams, where they told the young men and women all about the strangers who had been sent by the Great Manito; and in Hiawatha's lodge the strangers, weary from their journey and the summer heat, stretched themselves upon the robes of ermine and went fast asleep.

Slowly a coolness fell upon the air, and the rays of sunset gilded every thicket of the forest, when Hiawatha rose from his seat and whispered to Nokomis, saying: "O Nokomis, I am going on a long journey to the Land of Sunset and the home of the North-west wind. See that no harm comes to these guests, whom I leave here in your care. See that fear and danger or want of food and shelter never come near them in the lodge of Hiawatha."

Forth went Hiawatha into the village, and he bade farewell to all the warriors and to all the young men, saying to them: "My people, I am going on a distant journey, and many winters will have passed before I come once more among you. Listen to the truth my guests will tell you, for the Great Manito has sent them, and I leave them in your care. And now, farewell!" cried Hiawatha.

On the shore of the Big-Sea-Water for the last time Hiawatha launched his birch canoe, pushed it out from among the rushes and whispered to it, "Westward! Westward!" It darted forward like an arrow, and the rays of the setting sun shot a long and fiery pathway over the smooth waters of the lake.

Down this path of light sailed Hiawatha in his birch canoe right into the flaming sunset, and the Indians on the shore saw him moving on and on until he became a tiny speck against the splendor of the clouds. With a final lift and fall his canoe rose upon a sunbeam, and as it disappeared within the crimson sky the Indians all cried out: "Farewell, farewell, O Hiawatha!" And the trees in the forest, the waves on the edges of the lake and every living creature that ran or swam or flew took up the cry: "Farewell, Hiawatha!" For Hiawatha had disappeared forever in the kingdom of the North-west wind and the Islands of the Blessed.

THE SONG OF HIAWATHA

INTRODUCTION

SHOULD you ask me, whence these stories?
Whence these legends and traditions,
With the odors of the forest,
With the dew and damp of meadows,
With the curling smoke of wigwams,
With the rushing of great rivers,
With their frequent repetitions,
And their wild reverberations,
As of thunder in the mountains?
I should answer, I should tell you,
"From the forests and the prairies,
From the great lakes of the Northland,
From the land of the Ojibways,
From the land of the Dacotahs,
From the mountains, moors, and fen-lands,
Where the heron, the Shuh-shuh-gah,
Feeds among the reeds and rushes.
I repeat them as I heard them
From the lips of Nawadaha,
The musician, the sweet-singer."
Should you ask where Nawadaha
Found these songs, so wild and wayward,
Found these legends and traditions,
I should answer, I should tell you,
"In the bird's-nests of the forest,
In the lodges of the beaver,
In the hoof-prints of the bison,
In the eyry of the eagle!
"All the wild-fowl sang them to him,
In the moorlands and the fen-lands,
In the melancholy marshes;
Chetowaik, the plover, sang them,
Mahng, the loon, the wild-goose, Wawa,
The blue heron, the Shuh-shuh-gah,
And the grouse, the Mushkodasa!"
If still further you should ask me,
Saying, "Who was Nawadaha?
Tell us of this Nawadaha,"
I should answer your inquiries
Straightway in such words as follow.
"In the Vale of Tawasentha,
In the green and silent valley,
By the pleasant water-courses,
Dwelt the singer Nawadaha.
Round about the Indian village
Spread the meadows and the cornfields,
And beyond them stood the forest,
Stood the groves of singing pine-trees,
Green in Summer, white in Winter,
Ever sighing, ever singing.
"And the pleasant water-courses,

You could trace them through the valley,
By the rushing in the Spring-time,
By the alders in the Summer,
By the white fog in the Autumn,
By the black line in the Winter;
And beside them dwelt the singer,
In the Vale of Tawasentha,
In the green and silent valley.
"There he sang of Hiawatha,
Sang the song of Hiawatha,
Sang his wondrous birth and being,
How he prayed and how he fasted,
How he lived, and toiled, and suffered,
That the tribes of men might prosper,
That he might advance his people!"
Ye who love the haunts of Nature,
Love the sunshine of the meadow,
Love the shadow of the forest,
Love the wind among the branches,
And the rain-shower and the snow-storm,
And the rushing of great rivers
Through their palisades of pine-trees,
And the thunder in the mountains,
Whose innumerable echoes
Flap like eagles in their eyries;—
Listen to these wild traditions,
To this Song of Hiawatha!
Ye who love a nation's legends,
Love the ballads of a people,
That like voices from afar off
Call to us to pause and listen,
Speak in tones so plain and childlike
Scarcely can the ear distinguish
Whether they are sung or spoken;—
Listen to this Indian Legend,
To this song of Hiawatha!
Ye whose hearts are fresh and simple,
Who have faith in God and Nature,
Who believe, that in all ages
Every human heart is human,
That in even savage bosoms
There are longings, yearnings, strivings
For the good they comprehend not,
That the feeble hands and helpless,
Groping blindly in the darkness,
Touch God's right hand in that darkness
And are lifted up and strengthened;—
Listen to this simple story,
To this song of Hiawatha!
Ye, who sometimes in your rambles
Through the green lanes of the country,
Where the tangled barberry-bushes
Hang their tufts of crimson berries
Over stone walls gray with mosses,
Pause by some neglected graveyard,
For a while to muse, and ponder

On a half-effaced inscription,
Written with little skill of song-craft,
Homely phrases, but each letter
Full of hope, and yet of heart-break,
Full of all the tender pathos
Of the Here and the Hereafter;—
Stay and read this rude inscription,
Read this song of Hiawatha!

THE SONG OF HIAWATHA

I

THE PEACE-PIPE

ON the Mountains of the Prairie,
On the great Red Pipe-stone Quarry,
Gitche Manito, the mighty,
He the Master of Life, descending,
On the red crags of the quarry
Stood erect, and called the nations,
Called the tribes of men together.
From his footprints flowed a river,
Leaped into the light of morning,
O'er the precipice plunging downward
Gleamed like Ishkoodah, the comet.
And the Spirit, stooping earthward,
With his finger on the meadow
Traced a winding pathway for it,
Saying to it, "Run in this way!"
From the red stone of the quarry
With his hand he broke a fragment,
Molded it into a pipe-head,
Shaped and fashioned it with figures;
From the margin of the river
Took a long reed for a pipe-stem,
With its dark green leaves upon it;
Filled the pipe with bark of willow,
With the bark of the red willow;
Breathed upon the neighboring forest,
Made its great boughs chafe together,
Till in flame they burst and kindled;
And erect upon the mountains,
Gitche Manito, the mighty,
Smoked the calumet, the Peace-Pipe,
As a signal to the nations.
And the smoke rose slowly, slowly,
Through the tranquil air of morning,
First a single line of darkness,
Then a denser, bluer vapor,
Then a snow-white cloud unfolding,
Like the tree-tops of the forest,

Ever rising, rising, rising,
Till it touched the top of heaven,
Till it broke against the heaven,
And rolled outward all around it.
From the Vale of Tawasentha,
From the Valley of Wyoming,
From the groves of Tuscaloosa,
From the far-off Rocky Mountains,
From the Northern lakes and rivers
All the tribes beheld the signal,
Saw the distant smoke ascending
The Pukwana of the Peace-Pipe.
And the Prophets of the nations
Said: "Behold it, the Pukwana,
By this signal from afar off,
Bending like a wand of willow,
Waving like a hand that beckons,
Gitche Manito, the mighty,
Calls the tribes of men together,
Calls the warriors to his council!"
Down the rivers, o'er the prairies,
Came the warriors of the nations,
Came the Delawares and Mohawks,
Came the Choctaws and Comanches,
Came the Shoshonies and Blackfeet,
Came the Pawnees and Omahas,
Came the Mandans and Dacotahs,
Came the Hurons and Ojibways,
All the warriors drawn together
By the signal of the Peace-Pipe,
To the Mountains of the Prairie,
To the Great Red Pipe-stone Quarry.
And they stood there on the meadow
With their weapons and their war-gear
Painted like the leaves of Autumn,
Painted like the sky of morning,
Wildly glaring at each other;
In their faces stern defiance,
In their hearts the feuds of ages,
The hereditary hatred,
The ancestral thirst of vengeance.
Gitche Manito, the mighty,
The creator of the nations,
Looked upon them with compassion,
With paternal love and pity;
Looked upon their wrath and wrangling,
But as quarrels among children,
But as feuds and fights of children!
Over them he stretched his right hand,
To subdue their stubborn natures,
To allay their thirst and fever,
By the shadow of his right hand;
Spake to them with voice majestic
As the sound of far-off waters,
Falling into deep abysses,
Warning, chiding, spake in this wise:—

"O my children! my poor children!
Listen to the words of wisdom,
Listen to the words of warning,
From the lips of the Great Spirit,
From the Master of Life, who made you:
"I have given you lands to hunt in,
I have given you streams to fish in,
I have given you bear and bison,
I have given you roe and reindeer,
I have given you brant and beaver,
Filled the marshes full of wild-fowl,
Filled the rivers full of fishes;
Why then are you not contented?
Why then will you hunt each other?
"I am weary of your quarrels,
Weary of your wars and bloodshed.
Weary of your prayers for vengeance,
Of your wranglings and dissensions;
All your strength is in your union,
All your danger is in discord;
Therefore be at peace henceforward,
And as brothers live together.
"I will send a Prophet to you,
A Deliverer of the nations,
Who shall guide you and shall teach you,
Who shall toil and suffer with you.
If you listen to his counsels,
You will multiply and prosper;
If his warnings pass unheeded,
You will fade away and perish!
"Bathe now in the stream before you,
Wash the war-paint from your faces,
Wash the blood-stains from your fingers,
Bury your war-clubs and your weapons,
Break the red stone from this quarry,
Mold and make it into Peace-Pipes,
Take the reeds that grow beside you,
Deck them with your brightest feathers,
Smoke the calumet together,
And as brothers live henceforward!"
Then upon the ground the warriors
Threw their cloaks and shirts of deerskin,
Threw their weapons and their war-gear,
Leaped into the rushing river,
Washed the war-paint from their faces
Clear above them flowed the water,
Clear and limpid from the footprints
Of the Master of Life descending;
Dark below them flowed the water,
Soiled and stained with streaks of crimson,
As if blood were mingled with it!
From the river came the warriors,
Clean and washed from all their war-paint;
On the banks their clubs they buried,
Buried all their warlike weapons.
Gitche Manito, the mighty,

The Great Spirit, the creator,
Smiled upon his helpless children!
And in silence all the warriors
Broke the red stone of the quarry,
Smoothed and formed it into Peace-Pipes,
Broke the long reeds by the river,
Decked them with their brightest feathers,
And departed each one homeward,
While the Master of Life, ascending,
Through the opening of cloud-curtains,
Through the doorways of the heaven,
Vanished from before their faces,
In the smoke that rolled around him,
The Pukwana of the Peace-Pipe!

II

THE FOUR WINDS

"HONOR be to Mudjekeewis!"
Cried the warriors, cried the old men,
When he came in triumph homeward
With the sacred Belt of Wampum,
From the regions of the North-Wind,
From the kingdom of Wabasso,
From the land of the White Rabbit.
He had stolen the Belt of Wampum
From the neck of Mishe-Mokwa,
From the Great Bear of the mountains,
From the terror of the nations,
As he lay asleep and cumbrous
On the summit of the mountains,
Like a rock with mosses on it,
Spotted brown and gray with mosses.
Silently he stole upon him,
Till the red nails of the monster
Almost touched him, almost scared him,
Till the hot breath of his nostrils
Warmed the hands of Mudjekeewis,
As he drew the Belt of Wampum
Over the round ears, that heard not,
Over the small eyes, that saw not,
Over the long nose and nostrils,
The black muzzle of the nostrils,
Out of which the heavy breathing
Warmed the hands of Mudjekeewis.
Then he swung aloft his war-club,
Shouted loud and long his war-cry,
Smote the mighty Mishe-Mokwa
In the middle of the forehead,
Right between the eyes he smote him.
With the heavy blow bewildered,
Rose the Great Bear of the Mountains;
But his knees beneath him trembled,

And he whimpered like a woman,
As he reeled and staggered forward,
As he sat upon his haunches;
And the mighty Mudjekeewis,
Standing fearlessly before him,
Taunted him in loud derision,
Spake disdainfully in this wise:—
"Hark you, Bear! you are a coward,
And no Brave, as you pretended;
Else you would not cry and whimper
Like a miserable woman!
Bear! you know our tribes are hostile,
Long have been at war together;
Now you find that we are strongest,
You go sneaking in the forest,
You go hiding in the mountains!
Had you conquered me in battle
Not a groan would I have uttered;
But you, Bear! sit here and whimper,
And disgrace your tribe by crying,
Like a wretched Shaugodaya,
Like a cowardly old woman!"
Then again he raised his war-club,
Smote again the Mishe-Mokwa
In the middle of his forehead,
Broke his skull as ice is broken
When one goes to fish in Winter.
Thus was slain the Mishe-Mokwa,
He the Great Bear of the mountains,
He the terror of the nations.
"Honor be to Mudjekeewis!"
With a shout exclaimed the people,
"Honor be to Mudjekeewis!
Henceforth he shall be the West-Wind,
And hereafter and forever
Shall he hold supreme dominion
Over all the winds of heaven,
Call him no more Mudjekeewis,
Call him Kabeyun, the West-Wind!"
Thus was Mudjekeewis chosen
Father of the Winds of Heaven.
For himself he kept the West-Wind,
Gave the others to his children;
Unto Wabun gave the East-Wind,
Gave the South to Shawondasee,
And the North-Wind, wild and cruel,
To the fierce Kabibonokka.
Young and beautiful was Wabun;
He it was who brought the morning,
He it was whose silver arrows
Chased the dark o'er hill and valley;
He it was whose cheeks were painted
With the brightest streaks of crimson,
And whose voice awoke the village,
Called the deer and called the hunter.
Lonely in the sky was Wabun;

Though the birds sang gayly to him,
Though the wild-flowers of the meadow
Filled the air with odors for him,
Though the forests and the rivers
Sang and shouted at his coming,
Still his heart was sad within him,
For he was alone in heaven.
But one morning, gazing earthward,
While the village still was sleeping,
And the fog lay on the river,
Like a ghost, that goes at sunrise,
He beheld a maiden walking
All alone upon a meadow,
Gathering water-flags and rushes
By a river in the meadow.
Every morning gazing earthward,
Still the first thing he beheld there
Was her blue eyes looking at him,
Two blue lakes among the rushes.
And he loved the lonely maiden,
Who thus waited for his coming;
For they both were solitary,
She on earth and he in heaven.
And he wooed her with caresses,
Wooed her with his smile of sunshine,
With his flattering words he wooed her
With his sighing and his singing,
Gentlest whispers in the branches,
Softest music, sweetest odors,
Till he drew her to his bosom,
Folded in his robes of crimson,
Till into a star he changed her,
Trembling still upon his bosom;
And forever in the heavens
They are seen together walking,
Wabun and the Wabun-Annung,
Wabun and the Star of Morning.
But the fierce Kabibonokka
Had his dwelling among icebergs,
In the everlasting snow-drifts,
In the kingdom of Wabasso,
In the land of the White Rabbit.
He it was whose hand in Autumn
Painted all the trees with scarlet,
Stained the leaves with red and yellow;
He it was who sent the snow-flakes,
Sifting, hissing through the forest,
Froze the ponds, the lakes, the rivers,
Drove the loon and sea-gull southward,
Drove the cormorant and curlew
To their nests of sedge and sea-tang
In the realms of Shawondasee.
Once the fierce Kabibonokka
Issued from his lodge of snow-drifts,
From his home among the icebergs,
And his hair, with snow besprinkled,

Streamed behind him like a river,
Like a black and wintry river,
As he howled and hurried southward,
Over frozen lakes and moorlands.
There among the reeds and rushes
Found he Shingebis, the diver,
Trailing strings of fish behind him,
O'er the frozen fens and moorlands,
Lingering still among the moorlands,
Though his tribe had long departed
To the land of Shawondasee.
Cried the fierce Kabibonokka,
"Who is this that dares to brave me?
Dares to stay in my dominions,
When the Wawa has departed,
When the wild-goose has gone southward,
And the heron, the Shuh-shuh-gah,
Long ago departed southward?
I will go into his wigwam,
I will put his smouldering fire out!"
And at night Kabibonokka
To the lodge came wild and wailing,
Heaped the snow in drifts about it,
Shouted down into the smoke-flue,
Shook the lodge-poles in his fury,
Flapped the curtain of the doorway.
Shingebis, the diver, feared not,
Shingebis, the diver, cared not;
Four great logs had he for firewood,
One for each moon of the winter,
And for food the fishes served him.
By his blazing fire he sat there,
Warm and merry, eating, laughing,
Singing "O Kabibonokka,
You are but my fellow-mortal!"
Then Kabibonokka entered,
And though Shingebis, the diver,
Felt his presence by the coldness,
Felt his icy breath upon him,
Still he did not cease his singing,
Still he did not leave his laughing,
Only turned the log a little,
Only made the fire burn brighter,
Made the sparks fly up the smoke-flue.
From Kabibonokka's forehead,
From his snow-besprinkled tresses,
Drops of sweat fell fast and heavy,
Making dints upon the ashes,
As along the eves of lodges,
As from drooping boughs of hemlock,
Drips the melting snow in springtime,
Making hollows in the snow-drifts.
Till at last he rose defeated,
Could not bear the heat and laughter,
Could not bear the merry singing,
But rushed headlong through the doorway,

Stamped upon the crusted snow-drifts,
Stamped upon the lakes and rivers,
Made the snow upon them harder,
Made the ice upon them thicker,
Challenged Shingebis, the diver,
To come forth and wrestle with him,
To come forth and wrestle naked
On the frozen fens and moorlands.
Forth went Shingebis, the diver,
Wrestled all night with the North-Wind,
Wrestled naked on the moorlands
With the fierce Kabibonokka,
Till his panting breath grew fainter,
Till his frozen grasp grew feebler,
Till he reeled and staggered backward,
And retreated, baffled, beaten,
To the kingdom of Wabasso,
To the land of the White Rabbit,
Hearing still the gusty laughter,
Hearing Shingebis, the diver,
Singing, "O Kabibonokka,
You are but my fellow-mortal!"
Shawondasee, fat and lazy,
Had his dwelling far to southward,
In the drowsy, dreamy sunshine,
In the never-ending Summer.
He it was who sent the wood-birds,
Sent the Opechee, the robin,
Sent the blue bird, the Owaissa,
Sent the Shawshaw, sent the swallow,
Sent the wild-goose, Wawa, northward,
Sent the melons and tobacco,
And the grapes in purple clusters.
From his pipe the smoke ascending
Filled the sky with haze and vapor,
Filled the air with dreamy softness,
Gave a twinkle to the water,
Touched the rugged hills with smoothness,
Brought the tender Indian Summer
To the melancholy North-land,
In the dreary Moon of Snow-shoes.
Listless, careless Shawondasee!
In his life he had one shadow,
In his heart one sorrow had he.
Once, as he was gazing northward,
Far away upon a prairie
He beheld a maiden standing,
Saw a tall and slender maiden
All alone upon a prairie;
Brightest green were all her garments
And her hair was like the sunshine.
Day by day he gazed upon her,
Day by day he sighed with passion,
Day by day his heart within him
Grew more hot with love and longing
For the maid with yellow tresses.

But he was too fat and lazy
To bestir himself and woo her;
Yes, too indolent and easy
To pursue her and persuade her,
So he only gazed upon her,
Only sat and sighed with passion
For the maiden of the prairie.
Till one morning, looking northward,
He beheld her yellow tresses
Changed and covered o'er with whiteness,
Covered as with whitest snow-flakes.
"Ah! my brother from the North-land,
From the kingdom of Wabasso,
From the land of the White Rabbit!
You have stolen the maiden from me,
You have laid your hand upon her,
You have wooed and won my maiden,
With your stories of the North-land!"
Thus the wretched Shawondasee
Breathed into the air his sorrow;
And the South-Wind o'er the prairie
Wandered warm with sighs of passion
With the sighs of Shawondasee,
Till the air seemed full of snow-flakes,
Full of thistle-down the prairie,
And the maid with hair like sunshine
Vanished from his sight forever;
Never more did Shawondasee
See the maid with yellow tresses!
Poor, deluded Shawondasee!
'Twas no woman that you gazed at,
'Twas no maiden that you sighed for,
'Twas the prairie dandelion
That through all the dreamy Summer
You had gazed at with such longing,
You had sighed for with such passion,
And had puffed away forever,
Blown into the air with sighing.
Ah! deluded Shawondasee!
Thus the Four Winds were divided;
Thus the sons of Mudjekeewis
Had their stations in the heavens,
At the corners of the heavens;
For himself the West-Wind only
Kept the mighty Mudjekeewis.

III

HIAWATHA'S CHILDHOOD

DOWNWARD through the evening twilight,
In the days that are forgotten,
In the unremembered ages,
From the full moon fell Nokomis,

Fell the beautiful Nokomis.
She a wife, but not a mother.
She was sporting with her women,
Swinging in a swing of grape-vines,
When her rival, the rejected,
Full of jealousy and hatred,
Cut the leafy swing asunder,
Cut in twain the twisted grape-vines,
And Nokomis fell affrighted
Downward through the evening twilight,
On the Muskoday, the meadow,
On the prairie full of blossoms.
"See! a star falls!" said the people;
"From the sky a star is falling!"
There among the ferns and mosses,
There among the prairie lilies,
On the Muskoday, the meadow,
In the moonlight, and the starlight,
Fair Nokomis bore a daughter.
And she called her name Wenonah,
As the first-born of her daughters.
And the daughter of Nokomis
Grew up like the prairie lilies,
Grew a tall and slender maiden,
With the beauty of the moonlight,
With the beauty of the starlight.
And Nokomis warned her often,
Saying oft, and oft repeating,
"O, beware of Mudjekeewis,
Of the West-Wind, Mudjekeewis;
Listen not to what he tells you;
Lie not down upon the meadow,
Stoop not down among the lilies,
Lest the West-Wind come and harm you!"
But she heeded not the warning,
Heeded not those words of wisdom,
And the West-Wind came at evening,
Walking lightly o'er the prairie,
Whispering to the leaves and blossoms,
Bending low the flowers and grasses,
Found the beautiful Wenonah,
Lying there among the lilies,
Wooed her with his words of sweetness,
Wooed her with his soft caresses,
Till she bore a son in sorrow,
Bore a son of love and sorrow.
Thus was born my Hiawatha,
Thus was born the child of wonder;
But the daughter of Nokomis,
Hiawatha's gentle mother,
In her anguish died deserted
By the West-Wind, false and faithless,
By the heartless Mudjekeewis.
For her daughter, long and loudly
Wailed and wept the sad Nokomis;
"O that I were dead!" she murmured,

"O that I were dead, as thou art!
No more work, and no more weeping,
Wahonowin! Wahonowin!"
By the shores of Gitche Gumee,
By the shining Big-Sea-Water,
Stood the wigwam of Nokomis,
Daughter of the Moon, Nokomis.
Dark behind it rose the forest,
Rose the black and gloomy pine-trees,
Rose the firs with cones upon them;
Bright before it beat the water,
Beat the clear and sunny water,
Beat the shining Big-Sea-Water.
There the wrinkled, old Nokomis
Nursed the little Hiawatha,
Rocked him in his linden cradle,
Bedded soft in moss and rushes,
Safely bound with reindeer sinews;
Stilled his fretful wail by saying,
"Hush! the Naked Bear will get thee!"
Lulled him into slumber, singing,
"Ewa-yea! my little owlet!
Who is this, that lights the wigwam?
With his great eyes lights the wigwam?
Ewa-yea! my little owlet!"
Many things Nokomis taught him
Of the stars that shine in heaven;
Showed him Ishkoodah, the comet,
Ishkoodah, with fiery tresses;
Showed the Death-Dance of the spirits,
Warriors with their plumes and war-clubs,
Flaring far away to northward
In the frosty nights of Winter;
Showed the broad, white road in heaven,
Pathway of the ghosts, the shadows,
Running straight across the heavens,
Crowded with the ghosts, the shadows.
At the door on summer evenings
Sat the little Hiawatha;
Heard the whispering of the pine-trees,
Heard the lapping of the water,
Sounds of music, words of wonder;
"Minne-wawa!" said the pine-trees,
"Mudway aushka!" said the water.
Saw the fire-fly, Wah-wah-taysee,
Flitting through the dusk of evening,
With the twinkle of its candle
Lighting up the brakes and bushes,
And he sang the song of children,
Sang the song Nokomis taught him;
"Wah-wah-taysee, little fire-fly,
Little, flitting, white-fire insect,
Little, dancing, white-fire creature,
Light me with your little candle,
Ere upon my bed I lay me,
Ere in sleep I close my eyelids!"

Saw the moon rise from the water
Rippling, rounding from the water,
Saw the flecks and shadows on it,
Whispered, "What is that, Nokomis?'
And the good Nokomis answered:
"Once a warrior, very angry,
Seized his grandmother, and threw her
Up into the sky at midnight;
Right against the moon he threw her;
'Tis her body that you see there."
Saw the rainbow in the heaven,
In the eastern sky, the rainbow,
Whispered, "What is that, Nokomis?"
And the good Nokomis answered:
"'Tis the heaven of flowers you see there;
All the wild-flowers of the forest,
All the lilies of the prairie,
When on earth they fade and perish,
Blossom in that heaven above us."
When he heard the owls at midnight,
Hooting, laughing in the forest,
"What is that?" he cried in terror;
"What is that?" he said, "Nokomis?"
And the good Nokomis answered:
"That is but the owl and owlet,
Talking in their native language,
Talking, scolding at each other."
Then the little Hiawatha
Learned of every bird its language,
Learned their names and all their secrets,
How they built their nests in Summer,
Where they hid themselves in Winter,
Talked with them whene'er he met them,
Called them "Hiawatha's Chickens."
Of all beasts he learned the language,
Learned their names and all their secrets,
How the beavers built their lodges,
Where the squirrels hid their acorns,
How the reindeer ran so swiftly,
Why the rabbit was so timid,
Talked with them whene'er he met them,
Called them "Hiawatha's Brothers."
Then Iagoo, the great boaster,
He the marvellous story-teller,
He the traveller and the talker,
He the friend of old Nokomis,
Made a bow for Hiawatha;
From a branch of ash he made it,
From an oak-bough made the arrows,
Tipped with flint, and winged with feathers,
And the cord he made of deer-skin.
Then he said to Hiawatha:
"Go, my son, into the forest,
Where the red deer herd together,
Kill for us a famous roebuck,
Kill for us a deer with antlers!"

Forth into the forest straightway
All alone walked Hiawatha
Proudly, with his bow and arrows;
And the birds sang round him, o'er him,
"Do not shoot us, Hiawatha!"
Sang the Opechee, the robin,
Sang the bluebird, the Owaissa,
"Do not shoot us, Hiawatha!"
Up the oak-tree, close beside him,
Sprang the squirrel, Adjidaumo,
In and out among the branches,
Coughed and chattered from the oak-tree,
Laughed, and said between his laughing,
"Do not shoot me, Hiawatha!"
And the rabbit from his pathway
Leaped aside, and at a distance
Sat erect upon his haunches,
Half in fear and half in frolic,
Saying to the little hunter,
"Do not shoot me, Hiawatha!"
But he heeded not, nor heard them,
For his thoughts were with the red deer;
On their tracks his eyes were fastened,
Leading downward to the river,
To the ford across the river,
And as one in slumber walked he.
Hidden in the alder-bushes,
There he waited till the deer came,
Till he saw two antlers lifted,
Saw two eyes look from the thicket,
Saw two nostrils point to windward,
And a deer came down the pathway,
Flecked with leafy light and shadow.
And his heart within him fluttered,
Trembled like the leaves above him,
Like the birch-leaf palpitated,
As the deer came down the pathway.
Then upon one knee uprising,
Hiawatha aimed an arrow;
Scarce a twig moved with his motion,
Scarce a leaf was stirred or rustled,
But the wary roebuck started,
Stamped with all his hoofs together,
Listened with one foot uplifted,
Leaped as if to meet the arrow;
Ah! the singing, fatal arrow,
Like a wasp it buzzed and stung him!
Dead he lay there in the forest,
By the ford across the river;
Beat his timid heart no longer,
But the heart of Hiawatha
Throbbed and shouted and exulted,
As he bore the red deer homeward,
And Iagoo and Nokomis
Hailed his coming with applauses.
From the red deer's hide Nokomis

Made a cloak for Hiawatha,
From the red deer's flesh Nokomis
Made a banquet in his honor.
All the village came and feasted,
All the guests praised Hiawatha,
Called him Strong-Heart, Soan-ge-taha!
Called him Loon-Heart, Mahn-go-taysee!

IV

HIAWATHA AND MUDJEKEEWIS

OUT of childhood into manhood
Now had grown my Hiawatha,
Skilled in all the craft of hunters,
Learned in all the lore of old men,
In all youthful sports and pastimes,
In all manly arts and labors.
Swift of foot was Hiawatha;
He could shoot an arrow from him,
And run forward with such fleetness
That the arrow fell behind him!
Strong of arm was Hiawatha;
He could shoot ten arrows upward,
Shoot them with such strength and swiftness,
That the tenth had left the bow-string
Ere the first to earth had fallen!
He had mittens, Minjekahwun,
Magic mittens made of deer-skin;
When upon his hands he wore them,
He could smite the rocks asunder,
He could grind them into powder.
He had moccasins enchanted,
Magic moccasins of deer-skin;
When he bound them round his ankles,
When upon his feet he tied them,
At each stride a mile he measured!
Much he questioned old Nokomis
Of his father Mudjekeewis;
Learned from her the fatal secret
Of the beauty of his mother,
Of the falsehood of his father;
And his heart was hot within him,
Like a living coal his heart was.
Then he said to old Nokomis,
"I will go to Mudjekeewis,
See how fares it with my father,
At the door-ways of the West-Wind,
At the portals of the Sunset!"
From his lodge went Hiawatha,
Dressed for travel, armed for hunting;
Dressed in deer-skin shirt and leggings,
Richly wrought with quills and wampum;
On his head his eagle feathers,

Round his waist his belt of wampum,
In his hand his bow of ash-wood,
Strung with sinews of the reindeer;
In his quiver oaken arrows,
Tipped with jasper, winged with feathers;
With his mittens Minjekahwun,
With his moccasins enchanted.
Warning said the old Nokomis,
"Go not forth, O Hiawatha!
To the kingdom of the West-Wind,
To the realms of Mudjekeewis,
Lest he harm you with his magic,
Lest he kill you with his cunning!"
But the fearless Hiawatha
Heeded not her woman's warning;
Forth he strode into the forest,
At each stride a mile he measured;
Lurid seemed the sky above him,
Lurid seemed the earth beneath him,
Hot and close the air around him,
Filled with smoke and fiery vapors,
As of burning woods and prairies,
For his heart was hot within him,
Like a living coal his heart was.
So he journeyed westward, westward,
Left the fleetest deer behind him,
Left the antelope and bison;
Crossed the rushing Escanaba,
Crossed the mighty Mississippi,
Passed the Mountains of the Prairie,
Passed the land of Crows and Foxes,
Passed the dwellings of the Blackfeet,
Came unto the Rocky Mountains,
To the kingdom of the West-Wind,
Where upon the gusty summits
Sat the ancient Mudjekeewis,
Ruler of the winds of heaven.
Filled with awe was Hiawatha
At the aspect of his father
On the air about him wildly
Tossed and streamed the cloudy tresses,
Gleamed like drifting snow his tresses,
Glared like Ishkoodah, the comet,
Like the star with fiery tresses.
Filled with joy was Mudjekeewis
When he looked on Hiawatha,
Saw his youth rise up before him
In the face of Hiawatha,
Saw the beauty of Wenonah
From the grave rise up before him.
"Welcome!" said he, "Hiawatha,
To the kingdom of the West-Wind!
Long have I been waiting for you!
Youth is lovely, age is lonely,
Youth is fiery, age is frosty;
You bring back the days departed,

You bring back my youth of passion,
And the beautiful Wenonah!"
Many days they talked together,
Questioned, listened, waited, answered;
Much the mighty Mudjekeewis
Boasted of his ancient prowess,
Of his perilous adventures,
His indomitable courage,
His invulnerable body.
Patiently sat Hiawatha,
Listening to his father's boasting;
With a smile he sat and listened,
Uttered neither threat nor menace,
Neither word nor look betrayed him,
But his heart was hot within him,
Like a living coal his heart was.
Then he said, "O Mudjekeewis,
Is there nothing that can harm you?
Nothing that you are afraid of?"
And the mighty Mudjekeewis,
Grand and gracious in his boasting,
Answered saying, "There is nothing,
Nothing but the black rock yonder,
Nothing but the fatal Wawbeek?"
And he looked at Hiawatha
With a wise look and benignant,
With a countenance paternal,
Looked with pride upon the beauty
Of his tall and graceful figure,
Saying, "O my Hiawatha!
Is there anything can harm you?
Anything you are afraid of?"
But the wary Hiawatha
Paused awhile, as if uncertain,
Held his peace, as if resolving,
And then answered, "There is nothing,
Nothing but the bulrush yonder,
Nothing but the great Apukwa!"
And as Mudjekeewis, rising,
Stretched his hand to pluck the bulrush,
Hiawatha cried in terror,
Cried in well-dissembled terror,
"Kago! kago! do not touch it!"
"Ah, kaween!" said Mudjekeewis,
"No indeed, I will not touch it!"
Then they talked of other matters;
First of Hiawatha's brothers,
First of Wabun, of the East-Wind,
Of the South-Wind, Shawondasee,
Of the North Kabibonokka;
Then of Hiawatha's mother,
Of the beautiful Wenonah,
Of her birth upon the meadow,
Of her death, as old Nokomis
Had remembered and related.
And he cried, "O Mudjekeewis,

It was you who killed Wenonah,
Took her young life and her beauty,
Broke the Lily of the Prairie,
Trampled it beneath your footsteps;
You confess it! you confess it!"
And the Mighty Mudjekeewis
Tossed his gray hairs to the West-Wind,
Bowed his hoary head in anguish,
With a silent nod assented.
Then up started Hiawatha,
And with threatening look and gesture
Laid his hand upon the black rock,
On the fatal Wawbeek laid it,
With his mittens, Minjekahwun,
Rent the jutting crag asunder,
Smote and crushed it into fragments,
Hurled them madly at his father,
The remorseful Mudjekeewis,
For his heart was hot within him,
Like a living coal his heart was.
But the ruler of the West-Wind
Blew the fragments backward from him,
With the breathing of his nostrils,
With the tempest of his anger,
Blew them back at his assailant;
Seized the bulrush, the Apukwa,
Dragged it with its roots and fibres
From the margin of the meadow,
From its ooze, the giant bulrush;
Long and loud laughed Hiawatha!
Then began the deadly conflict,
Hand to hand among the mountains
From his eyry screamed the eagle,
The Keneu, the great war-eagle,
Sat upon the crags around them,
Wheeling flapped his wings above them.
Like a tall tree in the tempest
Bent and lashed the giant bulrush;
And in masses huge and heavy
Crashing fell the fatal Wawbeek;
Till the earth shook with the tumult
And confusion of the battle,
And the air was full of shoutings,
And the thunder of the mountains,
Starting, answered, "Baim-wawa!"
Back retreated Mudjekeewis,
Rushing westward o'er the mountains,
Stumbling westward down the mountains,
Three whole days retreated fighting,
Still pursued by Hiawatha
To the door-ways of the West-Wind,
To the portals of the Sunset,
To the earth's remotest border,
Where into the empty spaces
Sinks the sun, as a flamingo
Drops into her nest at nightfall,

In the melancholy marshes.
"Hold!" at length cried Mudjekeewis,
"Hold, my son, my Hiawatha!
'Tis impossible to kill me,
For you cannot kill the immortal.
I have put you to this trial,
But to know and prove your courage;
Now receive the prize of valor!
"Go back to your home and people,
Live among them, toil among them,
Cleanse the earth from all that harms it,
Clear the fishing-grounds and rivers,
Slay all monsters and magicians,
All the giants, the Wendigoes,
All the serpents, the Kenabeeks,
As I slew the Mishe-Mokwa.
Slew the Great Bear of the mountains.
"And at last when Death draws near you,
When the awful eyes of Pauguk
Glare upon you in the darkness,
I will share my kingdom with you,
Ruler shall you be henceforward
Of the Northwest-Wind, Keewaydin,
Of the home-wind, the Keewaydin."
Thus was fought that famous battle
In the dreadful days of Shah-shah,
In the days long since departed,
In the kingdom of the West-Wind.
Still the hunter sees its traces
Scattered far o'er hill and valley;
Sees the giant bulrush growing
By the ponds and water-courses,
Sees the masses of the Wawbeek
Lying still in every valley.
Homeward now went Hiawatha;
Pleasant was the landscape round him,
Pleasant was the air above him,
For the bitterness of anger
Had departed wholly from him,
From his brain the thought of vengeance,
From his heart the burning fever.
Only once his pace he slackened,
Only once he paused or halted,
Paused to purchase heads of arrows
Of the ancient Arrow-maker,
In the land of the Dacotahs,
Where the Falls of Minnehaha
Flash and gleam among the oak-trees,
Laugh and leap into the valley.
There the ancient Arrow-maker
Made his arrow-heads of sandstone,
Arrow-heads of chalcedony,
Arrow-heads of flint and jasper,
Smoothed and sharpened at the edges,
Hard and polished, keen and costly.
With him dwelt his dark-eyed daughter,

Wayward as the Minnehaha,
With her moods of shade and sunshine,
Eyes that smiled and frowned alternate,
Feet as rapid as the river,
Tresses flowing like the water,
And as musical a laughter;
And he named her from the river,
From the water-fall he named her,
Minnehaha, Laughing Water.
Was it then for heads of arrows,
Arrow-heads of chalcedony,
Arrow-heads of flint and jasper,
That my Hiawatha halted
In the land of the Dacotahs?
Was it not to see the maiden,
See the face of Laughing Water,
Peeping from behind the curtain,
Hear the rustling of her garments
From behind the waving curtain,
As one sees the Minnehaha
Gleaming, glancing through the branches,
As one hears the Laughing Water
From behind its screen of branches?
Who shall say what thoughts and visions
Fill the fiery brains of young men?
Who shall say what dreams of beauty
Filled the heart of Hiawatha?
All he told to old Nokomis,
When he reached the lodge at sunset,
Was the meeting with his father,
Was the fight with Mudjekeewis;
Not a word he said of arrows,
Not a word of Laughing Water.

V

HIAWATHA'S FASTING

YOU shall hear how Hiawatha
Prayed and fasted in the forest,
Not for greater skill in hunting,
Not for greater craft in fishing,
Not for triumphs in the battle,
And renown among the warriors
But for profit of the people,
For advantage of the nations.
First he built a lodge for fasting,
Built a wigwam in the forest,
By the shining Big-Sea-Water,
In the blithe and pleasant Spring-time,
In the Moon of Leaves he built it,
And, with dreams and visions many,
Seven whole days and nights he fasted.
On the first day of his fasting

Through the leafy woods he wandered;
Saw the deer start from the thicket,
Saw the rabbit in his burrow,
Heard the pheasant, Bena, drumming,
Heard the squirrel, Adjidaumo,
Rattling in his hoard of acorns,
Saw the pigeon, the Omeme,
Building nests among the pine-trees,
And in flocks the wild goose, Wawa,
Flying to the fen-lands northward,
Whirring, wailing far above him.
"Master of Life!" he cried, desponding,
"Must our lives depend on these things?"
On the next day of his fasting
By the river's brink he wandered,
Through the Muskoday, the meadow,
Saw the wild rice, Mahnomonee,
Saw the blueberry, Meenahga,
And the strawberry, Odahmin,
And the gooseberry, Shahbomin,
And the grape-vine, Bemahgut,
Trailing o'er the alder-branches,
Filling all the air with fragrance!
"Master of Life!" he cried, desponding,
"Must our lives depend on these things?"
On the third day of his fasting
By the lake he sat and pondered,
By the still, transparent water;
Saw the sturgeon, Nahma, leaping,
Scattering drops like beads of wampum
Saw the yellow perch, the Sahwa,
Like a sunbeam in the water,
Saw the pike, the Maskenozha,
And the herring, Okahahwis,
And the Shawgashee, the craw-fish!
"Master of Life!" he cried, desponding,
"Must our lives depend on these things?"
On the fourth day of his fasting
In his lodge he lay exhausted;
From his couch of leaves and branches,
Gazing with half-open eyelids,
Full of shadowy dreams and visions,
On the dizzy, swimming landscape,
On the gleaming of the water,
On the splendor of the sunset.
And he saw a youth approaching,
Dressed in garments green and yellow
Coming through the purple twilight,
Through the splendor of the sunset;
Plumes of green bent o'er his forehead,
And his hair was soft and golden.
Standing at the open doorway,
Long he looked at Hiawatha,
Looked with pity and compassion
On his wasted form and features,
And, in accents like the sighing

Of the South-Wind in the tree-tops,
Said he, "O my Hiawatha!
All your prayers are heard in heaven,
For you pray not like the others;
Not for greater skill in hunting,
Not for greater craft in fishing,
Not for triumph in the battle,
Nor renown among the warriors,
But for profit of the people,
For advantage of the nations.
"From the Master of Life descending,
I, the friend of man, Mondamin,
Come to warn you and instruct you,
How by struggle and by labor
You shall gain what you have prayed for.
Rise up from your bed of branches,
Rise, O youth, and wrestle with me!"
Faint with famine, Hiawatha
Started from his bed of branches,
From the twilight of his wigwam
Forth into the bush of sunset
Came, and wrestled with Mondamin;
At his touch he felt new courage
Throbbing in his brain and bosom,
Felt new life and hope and vigor
Run through every nerve and fibre.
So they wrestled there together
In the glory of the sunset,
And the more they strove and struggled,
Stronger still grew Hiawatha;
Till the darkness fell around them,
And the heron, the Shuh-shuh-gah,
From her haunts among the fen-lands,
Gave a cry of lamentation,
Gave a scream of pain and famine.
"'Tis enough!" then said Mondamin,
Smiling upon Hiawatha,
"But to-morrow, when the sun sets,
I will come again to try you."
And he vanished, and was seen not;
Whether sinking as the rain sinks,
Whether rising as the mists rise,
Hiawatha saw not, knew not,
Only saw that he had vanished,
Leaving him alone and fainting,
With the misty lake below him,
And the reeling stars above him.
On the morrow and the next day,
When the sun through heaven descending,
Like a red and burning cinder
From the hearth of the Great Spirit,
Fell into the western waters,
Came Mondamin for the trial,
For the strife with Hiawatha;
Came as silent as the dew comes,
From the empty air appearing,

Into empty air returning,
Taking shape when earth it touches,
But invisible to all men
In its coming and its going.
Thrice they wrestled there together
In the glory of the sunset,
Till the darkness fell around them,
Till the heron, the Shuh-shuh-gah,
From her haunts among the fen-lands,
Uttered her loud cry of famine,
And Mondamin paused to listen.
Tall and beautiful he stood there,
In his garments green and yellow;
To and fro his plumes above him
Waved and nodded with his breathing,
And the sweat of the encounter
Stood like drops of dew upon him.
And he cried, "O Hiawatha!
Bravely have you wrestled with me,
Thrice have wrestled stoutly with me,
And the Master of Life who sees us,
He will give to you the triumph!"
Then he smiled and said: "To-morrow
Is the last day of your conflict,
Is the last day of your fasting.
You will conquer and o'ercome me;
Make a bed for me to lie in,
Where the rain may fall upon me,
Where the sun may come and warm me;
Strip these garments, green and yellow,
Strip this nodding plumage from me,
Lay me in the earth, and make it
Soft and loose and light above me.
"Let no hand disturb my slumber,
Let no weed nor worm molest me,
Let not Kahgahgee, the raven,
Come to haunt me and molest me,
Only come yourself to watch me,
Till I wake, and start, and quicken,
Till I leap into the sunshine."
And thus saying, he departed;
Peacefully slept Hiawatha,
But he heard the Wawonaissa,
Heard the whippoorwill complaining,
Perched upon his lonely wigwam;
Heard the rushing Sebowisha,
Heard the rivulet rippling near him,
Talking to the darksome forest;
Heard the sighing of the branches,
As they lifted and subsided
At the passing of the night-wind,
Heard them, as one hears in slumber
Far-off murmurs, dreamy whispers:
Peacefully slept Hiawatha.
On the morrow came Nokomis,
On the seventh day of his fasting,

Came with food for Hiawatha,
Came imploring and bewailing,
Lest his hunger should o'ercome him,
Lest his fasting should be fatal.
But he tasted not and touched not,
Only said to her, "Nokomis,
Wait until the sun is setting,
Till the darkness falls around us,
Till the heron, the Shuh-shuh-gah,
Crying from the desolate marshes,
Tells us that the day is ended."
Homeward weeping went Nokomis,
Sorrowing for her Hiawatha,
Fearing lest his strength should fail him,
Lest his fasting should be fatal.
He meanwhile sat weary waiting
For the coming of Mondamin,
Till the shadows, pointing eastward,
Lengthened over field and forest,
Till the sun dropped from the heaven,
Floating on the waters westward,
As a red leaf in the Autumn
Falls and floats upon the water,
Falls and sinks into its bosom.
And behold! the young Mondamin,
With his soft and shining tresses,
With his garments green and yellow,
With his long and glossy plumage,
Stood and beckoned at the doorway.
And as one in slumber walking,
Pale and haggard, but undaunted,
From the wigwam Hiawatha
Came and wrestled with Mondamin.
Round about him spun the landscape,
Sky and forest reeled together,
And his strong heart leaped within him,
As the sturgeon leaps and struggles
In a net to break its meshes.
Like a ring of fire around him
Blazed and flared the red horizon,
And a hundred suns seemed looking
At the combat of the wrestlers.
Suddenly upon the greensward
All alone stood Hiawatha,
Panting with his wild exertion,
Palpitating with the struggle;
And before him, breathless, lifeless,
Lay the youth, with hair disheveled,
Plumage torn, and garments tattered,
Dead he lay there in the sunset.
And victorious Hiawatha
Made the grave as he commanded,
Stripped the garments from Mondamin,
Stripped his tattered plumage from him,
Laid him in the earth, and made it
Soft and loose and light above him;

And the heron, the Shuh-shuh-gah,
From the melancholy moorlands,
Gave a cry of lamentation,
Gave a cry of pain and anguish!
Homeward then went Hiawatha
To the lodge of old Nokomis,
And the seven days of his fasting
Were accomplished and completed.
But the place was not forgotten
Where he wrestled with Mondamin;
Nor forgotten nor neglected
Was the grave where lay Mondamin,
Sleeping in the rain and sunshine,
Where his scattered plumes and garments
Faded in the rain and sunshine.
Day by day did Hiawatha
Go to wait and watch beside it;
Kept the dark mold soft above it,
Kept it clean from weeds and insects,
Drove away, with scoffs and shoutings,
Kahgahgee, the king of ravens.
Till at length a small green feather
From the earth shot slowly upward,
Then another and another,
And before the Summer ended
Stood the maize in all its beauty,
With its shining robes about it,
And its long, soft, yellow tresses;
And in rapture Hiawatha
Cried aloud, "It is Mondamin!
Yes, the friend of man, Mondamin!"
Then he called to old Nokomis
And Iagoo, the great boaster,
Showed them where the maize was growing,
Told them of his wondrous vision,
Of his wrestling and his triumph,
Of this new gift to the nations,
Which should be their food forever.
And still later, when the Autumn
Changed the long, green leaves to yellow,
And the soft and juicy kernels
Grew like wampum hard and yellow,
Then the ripened ears he gathered,
Stripped the withered husks from off them,
As he once had stripped the wrestler,
Gave the first Feast of Mondamin,
And made known unto the people
This new gift of the Great Spirit.

VI

HIAWATHA'S FRIENDS

TWO good friends had Hiawatha
Singled out from all the others,
Bound to him in closest union,
And to whom he gave the right hand
Of his heart, in joy and sorrow;
Chibiabos, the musician,
And the very strong man, Kwasind.
Straight between them ran the pathway,
Never grew the grass upon it;
Singing birds, that utter falsehoods,
Story-tellers, mischief-makers,
Found no eager ear to listen,
Could not breed ill-will between them,
For they kept each other's counsel,
Spake with naked hearts together,
Pondering much and much contriving
How the tribes of men might prosper.
Most beloved by Hiawatha
Was the gentle Chibiabos,
He the best of all musicians,
He the sweetest of all singers.
Beautiful and childlike was he,
Brave as man is, soft as woman,
Pliant as a wand of willow,
Stately as a deer with antlers.
When he sang, the village listened;
All the warriors gathered round him,
All the women came to hear him;
Now he stirred their souls to passion,
Now he melted them to pity.
From the hollow reeds he fashioned
Flutes so musical and mellow,
That the brook, the Sebowisha,
Ceased to murmur in the woodland,
That the wood-birds ceased from singing,
And the squirrel, Adjidaumo,
Ceased his chatter in the oak-tree,
And the rabbit, the Wabasso,
Sat upright to look and listen.
Yes, the brook, the Sebowisha,
Pausing, said, "O Chibiabos,
Teach my waves to flow in music,
Softly as your words in singing!"
Yes, the bluebird, the Owaissa,
Envious, said, "O Chibiabos,
Teach me tones as wild and wayward,
Teach me songs as full of frenzy!"
Yes, the Opechee, the robin,
Joyous, said, "O Chibiabos,
Teach me songs as full of gladness!"
And the whippoorwill, Wawonaissa,
Sobbing, said, "O Chibiabos,
Teach me tones as melancholy,
Teach me songs as full of sadness!"

All the many sounds of nature
Borrowed sweetness from his singing;
All the hearts of men were softened
By the pathos of his music;
For he sang of peace and freedom,
Sang of beauty, love, and longing;
Sang of death, and life undying
In the Islands of the Blessed,
In the kingdom of Ponemah,
In the land of the Hereafter.
Very dear to Hiawatha
Was the gentle Chibiabos,
He the best of all musicians,
He the sweetest of all singers;
For his gentleness he loved him,
And the magic of his singing.
Dear, too, unto Hiawatha
Was the very strong man, Kwasind,
He the strongest of all mortals,
He the mightiest among many;
For his very strength he loved him,
For his strength allied to goodness.
Idle in his youth was Kwasind,
Very listless, dull, and dreamy,
Never played with other children,
Never fished and never hunted,
Not like other children was he;
But they saw that much he fasted,
Much his Manito entreated,
Much besought his Guardian Spirit.
"Lazy Kwasind!" said his mother,
"In my work you never help me!
In the Summer you are roaming
Idly in the fields and forests;
In the Winter you are cowering
O'er the firebrands in the wigwam!
In the coldest days of Winter
I must break the ice for fishing;
With my nets you never help me!
At the door my nets are hanging,
Dripping, freezing with the water:
Go and wring them, Yenadizze!
Go and dry them in the sunshine!"
Slowly, from the ashes, Kwasind
Rose, but made no angry answer;
From the lodge went forth in silence,
Took the nets, that hung together,
Dripping, freezing at the doorway,
Like a wisp of straw he wrung them,
Like a wisp of straw he broke them,
Could not wring them without breaking,
Such the strength was in his fingers.
"Lazy Kwasind!" said his father,
"In the hunt you never help me;
Every bow you touch is broken,
Snapped asunder every arrow;

54

Yet come with me to the forest,
You shall bring the hunting homeward."
Down a narrow pass they wandered,
Where a brooklet led them onward,
Where the trail of deer and bison
Marked the soft mud on the margin,
Till they found all further passage
Shut against them, barred securely
By the trunks of trees uprooted,
Lying lengthwise, lying crosswise,
And forbidding further passage.
"We must go back," said the old man,
"O'er these logs we cannot clamber;
Not a woodchuck could get through them,
Not a squirrel clamber o'er them!"
And straightway his pipe he lighted,
And sat down to smoke and ponder.
But before his pipe was finished,
Lo! the path was cleared before him;
All the trunks had Kwasind lifted,
To the right hand, to the left hand,
Shot the pine-trees swift as arrows,
Hurled the cedars light as lances.
"Lazy Kwasind!" said the young men,
As they sported in the meadow;
"Why stand idly looking at us,
Leaning on the rock behind you?
Come and wrestle with the others,
Let us pitch the quoit together!"
Lazy Kwasind made no answer,
To their challenge made no answer,
Only rose, and, slowly turning,
Seized the huge rock in his fingers,
Tore it from its deep foundation,
Poised it in the air a moment,
Pitched it sheer into the river,
Sheer into the swift Pauwating,
Where it still is seen in Summer.
Once as down that foaming river,
Down the rapids of Pauwating,
Kwasind sailed with his companions,
In the stream he saw a beaver,
Saw Ahmeek, the King of Beavers,
Struggling with the rushing currents,
Rising, sinking in the water.
Without speaking, without pausing,
Kwasind leaped into the river,
Plunged beneath the bubbling surface,
Through the whirlpools chased the beaver,
Followed him among the islands,
Stayed so long beneath the water,
That his terrified companions
Cried, "Alas! good-bye to Kwasind!
We shall never more see Kwasind!"
But he reappeared triumphant,
And upon his shining shoulders

Brought the beaver, dead and dripping
Brought the King of all the Beavers.
And these two, as I have told you,
Were the friends of Hiawatha,
Chibiabos, the musician,
And the very strong man, Kwasind.
Long they lived in peace together,
Spake with naked hearts together,
Pondering much and much contriving
How the tribes of men might prosper.

VII

HIAWATHA'S SAILING

"GIVE me of your bark, O Birch-Tree!
Of your yellow bark, O Birch-Tree!
Growing by the rushing river,
Tall and stately in the valley!
I a light canoe will build me,
Build a swift Cheemaun for sailing,
That shall float upon the river,
Like a yellow leaf in Autumn,
Like a yellow water-lily!
"Lay aside your cloak, O Birch-Tree!
Lay aside your white-skin wrapper,
For the Summer-time is coming,
And the sun is warm in heaven,
And you need no white-skin wrapper!"
Thus aloud cried Hiawatha
In the solitary forest,
By the rushing Taquamenaw,
When the birds were singing gayly,
In the Moon of Leaves were singing,
And the sun, from sleep awaking,
Started up and said, "Behold me!
Gheezis, the great Sun, behold me!"

"'GIVE ME OF YOUR ROOTS, O TAMARACK!'"—*Page*
164

And the tree with all its branches
Rustled in the breeze of morning,
Saying with a sigh of patience,
"Take my cloak, O Hiawatha!"
With his knife the tree he girdled;
Just beneath its lowest branches,
Just above the roots, he cut it,
Till the sap came oozing outward;
Down the trunk from top to bottom,
Sheer he cleft the bark asunder,
With a wooden wedge he raised it,
Stripped it from the trunk unbroken.
"Give me of your boughs, O Cedar!
Of your strong and pliant branches,
My canoe to make more steady,
Make more strong and firm beneath me!"
Through the summit of the Cedar,
Went a sound, a cry of horror,
Went a murmur of resistance;
But it whispered, bending downward,
"Take my boughs, O Hiawatha!"
Down he hewed the boughs of cedar,
Shaped them straightway to a framework,

57

Like two bows he formed and shaped them,
Like two bended bows together.
"Give me of your roots, O Tamarack!
Of your fibrous roots, O Larch-Tree!
My canoe to bind together.
So to bind the ends together,
That the water may not enter,
That the river may not wet me!"
And the Larch, with all its fibres,
Shivered in the air of morning,
Touched his forehead with its tassels,
Said, with one long sigh of sorrow,
"Take them all, O Hiawatha!"
From the earth he tore the fibres,
Tore the tough roots of the Larch-Tree,
Closely sewed the bark together,
Bound it closely to the framework.
Give me of your balm, O Fir-Tree!
Of your balsam and your resin,
So to close the seams together
That the water may not enter
That the river may not wet me!"
And the Fir-Tree, tall and sombre,
Sobbed through all its robes of darkness,
Rattled like a shore with pebbles,
Answered wailing, answered weeping,
"Take my balm, O Hiawatha!"
And he took the tears of balsam,
Took the resin of the Fir-Tree,
Smeared therewith each seam and fissure,
Made each crevice safe from water.
"Give me of your quills, O Hedgehog!
All your quills, O Kagh, the Hedgehog!
I will make a necklace of them,
Make a girdle for my beauty,
And two stars to deck her bosom!"
From a hollow tree the Hedgehog
With his sleepy eyes looked at him,
Shot his shining quills, like arrows,
Saying, with a drowsy murmur,
Through the tangle of his whiskers,
"Take my quills, O Hiawatha!"
From the ground the quills he gathered,
All the little shining arrows,
Stained them red and blue and yellow,
With the juice of roots and berries;
Into his canoe he wrought them,
Round its waist a shining girdle,
Round its bows a gleaming necklace,
On its breast two stars resplendent.
Thus the Birch Canoe was builded
In the valley, by the river,
In the bosom of the forest;
And the forest's life was in it,
All its mystery and its magic,
All the lightness of the birch-tree,

All the toughness of the cedar,
All the larch's supple sinews,
And it floated on the river
Like a yellow leaf in Autumn
Like a yellow water-lily.
Paddles none had Hiawatha,
Paddles none he had or needed,
For his thoughts as paddles served him,
And his wishes served to guide him;
Swift or slow at will he glided,
Veered to right or left at pleasure.
Then he called aloud to Kwasind,
To his friend, the strong man, Kwasind,
Saying, "Help me clear this river
Of its sunken logs and sand-bars."
Straight into the river Kwasind
Plunged as if he were an otter,
Dived as if he were a beaver,
Stood up to his waist in water,
To his arm-pits in the river,
Swam and shouted in the river,
Tugged at sunken logs and branches,
With his hands he scooped the sand-bars,
With his feet the ooze and tangle.
And thus sailed my Hiawatha
Down the rushing Taquamenaw,
Sailed through all its bends and windings,
Sailed through all its deeps and shallows,
While his friend, the strong man, Kwasind,
Swam the deeps, the shallows waded.
Up and down the river went they,
In and out among its islands,
Cleared its bed of root and sand-bar,
Dragged the dead trees from its channel,
Made its passage safe and certain,
Made a pathway for the people,
From its springs among the mountains,
To the water of Pauwating,
To the bay of Taquamenaw.

VIII

HIAWATHA'S FISHING

FORTH upon the Gitche Gumee,
On the shining Big-Sea-Water,
With his fishing-line of cedar,
Of the twisted bark of cedar,
Forth to catch the sturgeon Nahma,
Mishe-Nahma, King of Fishes,
In his birch canoe exulting
All alone went Hiawatha.
Through the clear, transparent water
He could see the fishes swimming

Far down in the depths below him;
See the yellow perch, the Sahwa,
Like a sunbeam in the water,
See the Shawgashee, the craw-fish,
Like a spider on the bottom,
On the white and sandy bottom.
At the stern sat Hiawatha,
With his fishing-line of cedar;
In his plumes the breeze of morning
Played as in the hemlock branches;
On the bows, with tail erected,
Sat the squirrel, Adjidaumo;
In his fur the breeze of morning
Played as in the prairie grasses.
On the white sand of the bottom
Lay the monster Mishe-Nahma,
Lay the sturgeon, King of Fishes;
Through his gills he breathed the water
With his fins he fanned and winnowed,
With his tail he swept the sand-floor.
There he lay in all his armor;
On each side a shield to guard him,
Plates of bone upon his forehead,
Down his sides and back and shoulders

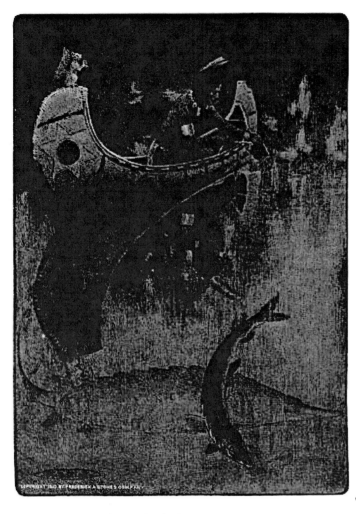

"TAKE MY BAIT, O KING OF FISHES!"—*Page 170*

Plates of bone with spines projecting!
Painted was he with his war-paints,
Stripes of yellow, red, and azure,
Spots of brown and spots of sable;
And he lay there on the bottom,
Fanning with his fins of purple,
As above him Hiawatha
In his birch canoe came sailing,
With his fishing-line of cedar.
"Take my bait," cried Hiawatha,
Down into the depths beneath him,
"Take my bait, O Sturgeon, Nahma!
Come up from below the water,
Let us see which is the stronger!"
And he dropped his line of cedar
Through the clear, transparent water,
Waited vainly for an answer,
Long sat waiting for an answer,
And repeating loud and louder,
"Take my bait, O King of Fishes!"
Quiet lay the sturgeon, Nahma,
Fanning slowly in the water,
Looking up at Hiawatha,
Listening to his call and clamor,

61

His unnecessary tumult,
Till he wearied of the shouting;
And he said to the Kenozha,
To the pike, the Maskenozha,
"Take the bait of this rude fellow,
Break the line of Hiawatha!"
In his fingers Hiawatha
Felt the loose line jerk and tighten;
As he drew it in, it tugged so
That the birch canoe stood endwise,
Like a birch log in the water,
With the squirrel, Adjidaumo,
Perched and frisking on the summit.
Full of scorn was Hiawatha
When he saw the fish rise upward,
Saw the pike, the Maskenozha,
Coming nearer, nearer to him,
And he shouted through the water,
"Esa! esa! shame upon you!
You are but the pike, Kenozha,
You are not the fish I wanted,
You are not the King of Fishes!"
Reeling downward to the bottom
Sank the pike in great confusion,
And the mighty sturgeon, Nahma,
Said to Ugudwash, the sun-fish,
"Take the bait of this great boaster,
Break the line of Hiawatha!"
Slowly upward, wavering, gleaming
Like a white moon in the water,
Rose the Ugudwash, the sun-fish,
Seized the line of Hiawatha,
Swung with all his weight upon it,
Made a whirlpool in the water,
Whirled the birch canoe in circles,
Round and round in gurgling eddies,
Till the circles in the water
Reached the far-off sandy beaches,
Till the water-flags and rushes
Nodded on the distant margins.
But when Hiawatha saw him
Slowly rising through the water,
Lifting his great disc of whiteness,
Loud he shouted in derision,
"Esa, esa! shame upon you!
You are Ugudwash, the sun-fish,
You are not the fish I wanted;
You are not the King of Fishes!"
Wavering downward, white and ghastly,
Sank the Ugudwash, the sun-fish,
And again the sturgeon, Nahma,
Heard the shout of Hiawatha,
Heard his challenge of defiance,
The unnecessary tumult,
Ringing far across the water.
From the white sand of the bottom

Up he rose with angry gesture,
Quivering in each nerve and fibre,
Clashing all his plates of armor,
Gleaming bright with all his war-paint;
In his wrath he darted upward,
Flashing leaped into the sunshine,
Opened his great jaws, and swallowed
Both canoe and Hiawatha.
Down into that darksome cavern
Plunged the headlong Hiawatha,
As a log on some black river
Shoots and plunges down the rapids,
Found himself in utter darkness,
Groped about in helpless wonder,
Till he felt a great heart beating,
Throbbing in that utter darkness.
And he smote it in his anger,
With his fist, the heart of Nahma,
Felt the mighty King of Fishes
Shudder through each nerve and fibre,
Heard the water gurgle round him
As he leaped and staggered through it,
Sick at heart, and faint and weary.
Crosswise then did Hiawatha,
Drag his birch-canoe for safety,
Lest from out the jaws of Nahma,
In the turmoil and confusion,
Forth he might be hurled and perish.
And the squirrel, Adjidaumo,
Frisked and chattered very gayly,
Toiled and tugged with Hiawatha
Till the labor was completed.
Then said Hiawatha to him,
"O my little friend, the squirrel,
Bravely have you toiled to help me;
Take the thanks of Hiawatha,
And the name which now he gives you;
For hereafter and forever
Boys shall call you Adjidaumo,
Tail-in-air the boys shall call you!"
And again the sturgeon, Nahma,
Gasped and quivered in the water,
Then was still, and drifted landward
Till he grated on the pebbles,
Till the listening Hiawatha
Heard him grate upon the margin,
Felt him strand upon the pebbles,
Knew that Nahma, King of Fishes,
Lay there dead upon the margin.
Then he heard a clang and flapping,
As of many wings assembling,
Heard a screaming and confusion,
As of birds of prey contending,
Saw a gleam of light above him,
Shining through the ribs of Nahma,
Saw the glittering eyes of sea-gulls,

Of Kayoshk, the sea-gulls, peering,
Gazing at him through the opening,
Heard them saying to each other,
"'Tis our brother, Hiawatha!"
And he shouted from below them,
Cried exulting from the caverns:
"O ye sea-gulls! O my brothers!
I have slain the sturgeon, Nahma;
Make the rifts a little larger,
With your claws the openings widen,
Set me free from this dark prison,
And henceforward and forever
Men shall speak of your achievements,
Calling you Kayoshk, the sea-gulls,
Yes, Kayoshk, the Noble Scratchers!"
And the wild and clamorous sea-gulls
Toiled with beak and claws together,
Made the rifts and openings wider
In the mighty ribs of Nahma,
And from peril and from prison,
From the body of the sturgeon,
From the peril of the water,
Was released my Hiawatha.
He was standing near his wigwam,
On the margin of the water,
And he called to old Nokomis,
Called and beckoned to Nokomis,
Pointed to the sturgeon, Nahma,
Lying lifeless on the pebbles,
With the sea-gulls feeding on him.
"I have slain the Mishe-Nahma,
Slain the King of Fishes!" said he;
"Look! the sea-gulls feed upon him,
Yes, my friends Kayoshk, the sea-gulls;
Drive them not away, Nokomis,
They have saved me from great peril
In the body of the sturgeon,
Wait until their meal is ended,
Till their craws are full with feasting,
Till they homeward fly, at sunset,
To their nests among the marshes;
Then bring all your pots and kettles,
And make oil for us in Winter."
And she waited till the sun set,
Till the pallid moon, the Night-sun,
Rose above the tranquil water,
Till Kayoshk, the sated sea-gulls,
From their banquet rose with clamor,
And across the fiery sunset
Winged their way to far-off islands,
To their nests among the rushes.
To his sleep went Hiawatha,
And Nokomis to her labor,
Toiling patient in the moonlight,
Till the sun and moon changed places,
Till the sky was red with sunrise,

And Kayoshk, the hungry sea-gulls,
Came back from the reedy islands,
Clamorous for their morning banquet.
Three whole days and nights alternate
Old Nokomis and the sea-gulls
Stripped the oily flesh of Nahma,
Till the waves washed through the rib-bones,
Till the sea-gulls came no longer,
And upon the sands lay nothing
But the skeleton of Nahma.

IX

HIAWATHA AND THE PEARL-FEATHER

ON the shores of Gitche Gumee,
Of the shining Big-Sea-Water,
Stood Nokomis, the old woman,
Pointing with her finger westward,
O'er the water pointing westward,
To the purple clouds of sunset.
Fiercely the red sun descending
Burned his way along the heavens,
Set the sky on fire behind him,
As war-parties, when retreating,
Burn the prairies on their war-trail;
And the moon, the Night-sun, eastward,
Suddenly starting from his ambush,
Followed fast those bloody footprints,
Followed in that fiery war-trail,
With its glare upon his features.
And Nokomis, the old woman,
Pointing with her finger westward,
Spake these words to Hiawatha:
"Yonder dwells the great Pearl-Feather,
Megissogwon, the Magician,
Manito of Wealth and Wampum,
Guarded by his fiery serpents,
Guarded by the black pitch-water.
You can see his fiery serpents,
The Kenabeek, the great serpents,
Coiling, playing in the water;
You can see the black pitch-water
Stretching far away beyond them,
To the purple clouds of sunset!
"He it was who slew my father,
By his wicked wiles and cunning,
When he from the moon descended,
When he came on earth to seek me
He, the mightiest of Magicians,
Sends the fever from the marshes,
Sends the pestilential vapors,
Sends the poisonous exhalations,

Sends the white fog from the fen-lands,
Sends disease and death among us!
"Take your bow, O Hiawatha,
Take your arrows, jasper-headed,
Take your war-club, Puggawaugun,
And your mittens, Minjekahwun,
And your birch-canoe for sailing,
And the oil of Mishe-Nahma,
So to smear its sides, that swiftly
You may pass the black pitch-water;
Slay this merciless magician,
Save the people from the fever
That he breathes across the fen-lands,
And avenge my father's murder!"
Straightway then my Hiawatha
Armed himself with all his war-gear,
Launched his birch-canoe for sailing;
With his palm its sides he patted,
Said with glee, "Cheemaun, my darling,
O my Birch-Canoe! leap forward,
Where you see the fiery serpents,
Where you see the black pitch-water!"
Forward leaped Cheemaun exulting,
And the noble Hiawatha
Sang his war-song wild and woeful,
And above him the war-eagle,
The Keneu, the great war-eagle,
Master of all fowls with feathers,
Screamed and hurtled through the heavens.
Soon he reached the fiery serpents,
The Kenabeek, the great serpents,
Lying huge upon the water,
Sparkling, rippling in the water,
Lying coiled across the passage,
With their blazing crests uplifted,
Breathing fiery fogs and vapors,
So that none could pass beyond them.
But the fearless Hiawatha
Cried aloud, and spake in this wise:
"Let me pass my way, Kenabeek,
Let me go upon my journey!"
And they answered, hissing fiercely,
With their fiery breath made answer,
"Back, go back! O Shaugodaya!
Back to old Nokomis, Faint-heart!"
Then the angry Hiawatha
Raised his mighty bow of ash-tree,
Seized his arrows, jasper-headed,
Shot them fast among the serpents;
Every twanging of the bow-string
Was a war-cry and a death-cry,
Every whizzing of an arrow
Was a death-song of Kenabeek.
Weltering in the bloody water,
Dead lay all the fiery serpents,
And among them Hiawatha

Harmless sailed, and cried exulting:
"Onward, O Cheemaun, my darling!
Onward to the black pitch-water!"
Then he took the oil of Nahma,
And the bows and sides anointed,
Smeared them well with oil, that swiftly
He might pass the black pitch-water,
All night long he sailed upon it,
Sailed upon that sluggish water,
Covered with its mould of ages,
Black with rotting water-rushes,
Rank with flags and leaves of lilies,
Stagnant, lifeless, dreary, dismal,
Lighted by the shimmering moonlight,
And by will-o'-the-wisps illumined,
Fires by ghosts of dead men kindled,
In their weary night-encampments.
All the air was white with moonlight,
All the water black with shadow,
And around him the Suggema,
The mosquito, sang their war-song,
And the fire-flies, Wah-wah-taysee,
Waved their torches to mislead him;
And the bull-frog, the Dahinda,
Thrust his head into the moonlight,
Fixed his yellow eyes upon him,
Sobbed and sank beneath the surface;
And anon a thousand whistles,
Answered over all the fen-lands,
And the heron, the Shuh-shuh-gah,
Far off on the reedy margin,
Heralded the hero's coming.
Westward thus fared Hiawatha,
Toward the realm of Megissogwon,
Towards the land of the Pearl-Feather,
Till the level moon stared at him,
In his face stared pale and haggard,
Till the sun was hot behind him,
Till it burned upon his shoulders,
And before him on the upland
He could see the Shining Wigwam
Of the Manito of Wampum,
Of the mightiest of Magicians.
Then once more Cheemaun he patted,
To his birch-canoe said, "Onward!"
And it stirred in all its fibres,
And with one great bound of triumph
Leaped across the water lilies,
Leaped through tangled flags and rushes,
And upon the beach beyond them
Dry-shod landed Hiawatha.
Straight he took his bow of ash-tree,
One end on the sand he rested,
With his knee he pressed the middle,
Stretched the faithful bow-string tighter.
Took an arrow, jasper-headed,

Shot it at the Shining Wigwam,
Sent it singing as a herald,
As a bearer of his message,
Of his challenge loud and lofty:
"Come forth from your lodge, Pearl-Feather!
Hiawatha waits your coming!"
Straightway from the Shining Wigwam
Came the mighty Megissogwon,
Tall of stature, broad of shoulder,
Dark and terrible in aspect,
Clad from head to foot in wampum,
Armed with all his warlike weapons,
Painted like the sky of morning,
Streaked with crimson, blue, and yellow,
Crested with great eagle-feathers,
Streaming upward, streaming outward.
"Well I know you, Hiawatha!"
Cried he in a voice of thunder,
In a tone of loud derision.
"Hasten back, O Shaugodaya!
Hasten back among the women,
Back to old Nokomis, Faint-heart,
I will slay you as you stand there,
As of old I slew her father!"
But my Hiawatha answered,
Nothing daunted, fearing nothing:
"Big words do not smite like war clubs,
Boastful breath is not a bow-string,
Taunts are not so sharp as arrows,
Deeds are better things than words are,
Actions mightier than boastings!"
Then began the greatest battle
That the sun had ever looked on,
That the war-birds ever witnessed.
All a Summer's day it lasted,
From the sunrise to the sunset;
For the shafts of Hiawatha,
Harmless hit the shirt of wampum,
Harmless fell the blows he dealt it
With his mittens, Minjekahwun,
Harmless fell the heavy war-club;
It could dash the rocks asunder,
But it could not break the meshes
Of that magic shirt of wampum.
Till at sunset Hiawatha,
Leaning on his bow of ash-tree,
Wounded, weary, and desponding,
With his mighty war-club broken,
With his mittens torn and tattered,
And three useless arrows only,
Paused to rest beneath a pine-tree,
From whose branches trailed the mosses,
And whose trunk was coated over
With the Dead-man's Moccasin-leather,
With the fungus white and yellow.
Suddenly from the boughs above him

Sang the Mama, the woodpecker:
"Aim your arrows, Hiawatha,
At the head of Megissogwon,
Strike the tuft of hair upon it,
At their roots the long black tresses;
There alone can he be wounded!"
Winged with feathers, tipped with jasper,
Swift flew Hiawatha's arrow,
Just as Megissogwon, stooping,
Raised a heavy stone to throw it.
Full upon the crown it struck him,
At the roots of his long tresses,
And he reeled and staggered forward,
Plunging like a wounded bison,
Yes, like Pezhekee, the bison,
When the snow is on the prairie.
Swifter flew the second arrow,
In the pathway of the other,
Piercing deeper than the other,
Wounding sorer than the other,
And the knees of Megissogwon
Shook like windy reeds beneath him,
Bent and trembled like the rushes.
But the third and latest arrow
Swiftest flew, and wounded sorest,
And the mighty Megissogwon
Saw the fiery eyes of Pauguk,
Saw the eyes of Death glare at him,
Heard his voice call in the darkness;
At the feet of Hiawatha
Lifeless lay the great Pearl-Feather,
Lay the mightiest of Magicians.
Then the grateful Hiawatha
Called the Mama, the woodpecker,
From his perch among the branches
Of the melancholy pine-tree,
And, in honor of his service,
Stained with blood the tuft of feathers
On the little head of Mama;
Even to this day he wears it,
Wears the tuft of crimson feathers,
As a symbol of his service.
Then he stripped the shirt of wampum
From the back of Megissogwon,
As a trophy of the battle,
As a signal of his conquest.
On the shore he left the body,
Half on land and half in water,
In the sand his feet were buried,
And his face was in the water.
And above him, wheeled and clamored
The Keneu, the great war-eagle,
Sailing round in narrower circles,
Hovering nearer, nearer, nearer.
From the wigwam Hiawatha
Bore the wealth of Megissogwon,

All his wealth of skins and wampum,
Furs of bison and of beaver,
Furs of sable and of ermine,
Wampum belts and strings and pouches,
Quivers wrought with beads of wampum,
Filled with arrows, silver-headed.
Homeward then he sailed exulting,
Homeward through the black pitch-water,
Homeward through the weltering serpents,
With the trophies of the battle,
With a shout and song of triumph.
On the shore stood old Nokomis,
On the shore stood Chibiabos,
And the very strong man, Kwasind,
Waiting for the hero's coming,
Listening to his song of triumph.
And the people of the village
Welcomed him with songs and dances,
Made a joyous feast, and shouted,
"Honor be to Hiawatha!
He has slain the great Pearl-Feather,
Slain the mightiest of Magicians,
Him, who sent the fiery fever,
Sent the white fog from the fen-lands,
Sent disease and death among us!"
Ever dear to Hiawatha
Was the memory of Mama!
And in token of his friendship,
As a mark of his remembrance,
He adorned and decked his pipe-stem
With the crimson tuft of feathers,
With the blood-red crest of Mama.
But the wealth of Megissogwon,
All the trophies of the battle,
He divided with his people,
Shared it equally among them.

X

HIAWATHA'S WOOING

"As unto the bow the cord is,
So unto the man is woman,
Though she bends him, she obeys him,
Though she draws him, yet she follows,
Useless each without the other!"
Thus the youthful Hiawatha
Said within himself and pondered,
Much perplexed by various feelings,
Listless, longing, hoping, fearing,
Dreaming still of Minnehaha,
Of the lovely Laughing Water,
In the land of the Dacotahs.
"Wed a maiden of your people,"

Warning said the old Nokomis;
"Go not eastward, go not westward,
For a stranger, whom we know not!
Like a fire upon the hearth-stone
Is a neighbor's homely daughter,
Like the starlight or the moonlight
Is the handsomest of strangers!"
Thus dissuading spake Nokomis,
And my Hiawatha answered
Only this: "Dear old Nokomis,
Very pleasant is the firelight,
But I like the starlight better,
Better do I like the moonlight!"
Gravely then said old Nokomis:
"Bring not here an idle maiden,
Bring not here a useless woman,
Hands unskilful, feet unwilling;
Bring a wife with nimble fingers,
Heart and hand that move together,
Feet that run on willing errands!"
Smiling answered Hiawatha:
"In the land of the Dacotahs
Lives the Arrow-maker's daughter,
Minnehaha, Laughing Water,
Handsomest of all the women.
I will bring her to your wigwam,
She shall run upon your errands,
Be your starlight, moonlight, firelight,
Be the sunlight of my people!"
Still dissuading said Nokomis:
"Bring not to my lodge a stranger
From the land of the Dacotahs!
Very fierce are the Dacotahs,
Often is there war between us,
There are feuds yet unforgotten,
Wounds that ache and still may open!"
Laughing answered Hiawatha:
"For that reason, if no other,
Would I wed the fair Dacotah,
That our tribes might be united,
That old feuds might be forgotten,
And old wounds be healed forever!"
Thus departed Hiawatha
To the land of the Dacotahs,
To the land of handsome women;
Striding over moor and meadow,
Through interminable forests,
Through uninterrupted silence.
With his moccasins of magic,
At each stride a mile he measured;
Yet the way seemed long before him,
And his heart outran his footsteps;
And he journeyed without resting,
Till he heard the cataract's thunder,
Heard the falls of Minnehaha,
Calling to him through the silence.

"Pleasant is the sound!" he murmured,
"Pleasant is the voice that calls me!"
On the outskirts of the forest,
'Twixt the shadow and the sunshine,
Herds of fallow deer were feeding,
But they saw not Hiawatha;
To his bow he whispered, "Fail not!"
To his arrow whispered, "Swerve not!"
Sent it singing on its errand,
To the red heart of the roebuck;
Threw the deer across his shoulder,
And sped forward without pausing.
At the doorway of his wigwam
Sat the ancient Arrow-maker,
In the land of the Dacotahs,
Making arrow-heads of jasper,
Arrow-heads of chalcedony.
At his side, in all her beauty,
Sat the lovely Minnehaha,
Sat his daughter, Laughing Water,
Plaiting mats of flags and rushes;
Of the past the old man's thoughts were,
And the maiden's of the future.
He was thinking, as he sat there,
Of the days when with such arrows,
He had struck the deer and bison,
On the Muskoday, the meadow;
Shot the wild goose, flying southward
On the wing, the clamorous Wawa;
Thinking of the great war-parties,
How they came to buy his arrows,
Could not fight without his arrows.
Ah, no more such noble warriors
Could be found on earth as they were!
Now the men were all like women,
Only used their tongues for weapons!
She was thinking of a hunter,
From another tribe and country,
Young and tall and very handsome,
Who one morning, in the Spring-time,
Came to buy her father's arrows,
Sat and rested in the wigwam,
Lingered long about the doorway,
Looking back as he departed.
She had heard her father praise him,
Praise his courage and his wisdom;
Would he come again for arrows
To the Falls of Minnehaha?
On the mat her hands lay idle,
And her eyes were very dreamy.
Through their thoughts they heard a footstep,
Heard a rustling in the branches,
And with glowing cheek and forehead,
With the deer upon his shoulders,
Suddenly from out the woodlands
Hiawatha stood before them.

Straight the ancient Arrow-maker
Looked up gravely from his labor,
Laid aside the unfinished arrow,
Bade him enter at the doorway,
Saying, as he rose to meet him,
"Hiawatha, you are welcome!"
At the feet of Laughing Water
Hiawatha laid his burden,
Threw the red deer from his shoulders;
And the maiden looked up at him,
Looked up from her mat of rushes,
Said with gentle look and accent,
"You are welcome, Hiawatha!"
Very spacious was the wigwam,
Made of deer-skin dressed and whitened,
With the Gods of the Dacotahs
Drawn and painted on its curtains
And so tall the doorway, hardly
Hiawatha stooped to enter,
Hardly touched his eagle-feathers
As he entered at the doorway.
Then uprose the Laughing Water,
From the ground fair Minnehaha
Laid aside her mat unfinished,
Brought forth food and set before them,
Water brought them from the brooklet,
Gave them food in earthen vessels,
Gave them drink in bowls of basswood,
Listened while the guest was speaking,
Listened while her father answered
But not once her lips she opened,
Not a single word she uttered.
Yes, as in a dream she listened
To the words of Hiawatha,
As he talked of old Nokomis,
Who had nursed him in his childhood,
As he told of his companions,
Chibiabos, the musician,
And the very strong man, Kwasind,
And of happiness and plenty
In the land of the Ojibways,
In the pleasant land and peaceful.
"After many years of warfare,
Many years of strife and bloodshed,
There is peace between the Ojibways
And the tribes of the Dacotahs."
Thus continued Hiawatha,
And then added, speaking slowly,
"That this peace may last forever
And our hands be clasped more closely,
And our hearts be more united,
Give me as my wife this maiden,
Minnehaha, Laughing Water,
Loveliest of Dacotah women!"
And the ancient Arrow-maker
Paused a moment ere he answered,

Smoked a little while in silence,
Looked at Hiawatha proudly,
Fondly looked at Laughing Water,
And made answer very gravely:
"Yes, if Minnehaha wishes;
Let your heart speak, Minnehaha!"
And the lovely Laughing Water
Seemed more lovely, as she stood there,
Neither willing nor reluctant,
As she went to Hiawatha,
Softly took the seat beside him,
While she said, and blushed to say it,
"I will follow you, my husband!"
This was Hiawatha's wooing!
Thus it was he won the daughter
Of the ancient Arrow-maker,
In the land of the Dacotahs!
From the wigwam he departed,
Leading with him Laughing Water;
Hand in hand they went together,
Through the woodland and the meadow,
Left the old man standing lonely
At the doorway of his wigwam,
Heard the Falls of Minnehaha
Calling to them from the distance,
Crying to them from afar off,
"Fare thee well, O Minnehaha!"
And the ancient Arrow-maker
Turned again unto his labor,
Sat down by his sunny doorway,
Murmuring to himself, and saying:
"Thus it is our daughters leave us,
Those we love, and those who love us!
Just when they have learned to help us,
When we are old and lean upon them,
Comes a youth with flaunting feathers,
With his flute of reeds, a stranger
Wanders piping through the village,
Beckons to the fairest maiden,
And she follows where he leads her,
Leaving all things for the stranger!"
Pleasant was the journey homeward,
Through interminable forests,
Over meadow, over mountain,
Over river, hill, and hollow.
Short it seemed to Hiawatha,
Though they journeyed very slowly,
Though his pace he checked and slackened
To the steps of Laughing Water.
Over wide and rushing rivers
In his arms he bore the maiden;
Light he thought her as a feather,
As the plume upon his head-gear;
Cleared the tangled pathway for her,
Bent aside the swaying branches,
Made at night a lodge of branches,

And a bed with boughs of hemlock,
And a fire before the doorway
With the dry cones of the pine-tree.
All the traveling winds went with them,
O'er the meadow, through the forest;
All the stars of night looked at them,
Watched with sleepless eyes their slumber;
From his ambush in the oak-tree
Peeped the squirrel, Adjidaumo,
Watched with eager eyes the lovers;
And the rabbit, the Wabasso,
Scampered from the path before them,
Peering, peeping from his burrow,
Sat erect upon his haunches,
Watched with curious eyes the lovers.
Pleasant was the journey homeward!
All the birds sang loud and sweetly
Songs of happiness and heart's-ease;
Sang the bluebird, the Owaissa,
"Happy are you, Hiawatha,
Having such a wife to love you!"
Sang the Opechee, the robin,
"Happy are you, Laughing Water,
Having such a noble husband!"
From the sky the sun benignant
Looked upon them through the branches,
Saying to them, "O my children,
Love is sunshine, hate is shadow,
Life is checkered shade and sunshine,
Rule by love, O Hiawatha!"
From the sky the moon looked at them,
Filled the lodge with mystic splendors,
Whispered to them, "O my children,
Day is restless, night is quiet,
Man imperious, woman feeble;
Half is mine, although I follow;
Rule by patience, Laughing Water!"
Thus it was they journeyed homeward;
Thus it was that Hiawatha
To the lodge of old Nokomis
Brought the moonlight, starlight, firelight,
Brought the sunshine of his people,
Minnehaha, Laughing Water,
Handsomest of all the women
In the land of the Dacotahs,
In the land of handsome women.

XI

HIAWATHA'S WEDDING FEAST

YOU shall hear how Pau-Puk-Keewis,
How the handsome Yenadizze
Danced at Hiawatha's wedding;

How the gentle Chibiabos,
He the sweetest of musicians,
Sang his songs of love and longing;
How Iagoo, the great boaster,
He the marvelous story-teller,
Told his tales of strange adventure,
That the feast might be more joyous,
That the time might pass more gayly,
And the guests be more contented.
Sumptuous was the feast Nokomis
Made at Hiawatha's wedding;
All the bowls were made of basswood,
White and polished very smoothly,
All the spoons of horn of bison,
Black and polished very smoothly.
She had sent through all the village
Messengers with wands of willow,
As a sign of invitation,
As a token of the feasting;
And the wedding guests assembled,
Clad in all their richest raiment,
Robes of fur and belts of wampum,
Splendid with their paint and plumage,
Beautiful with beads and tassels.
First they ate the sturgeon, Nahma,
And the pike, the Maskenozha,
Caught and cooked by old Nokomis;
Then on pemican they feasted,
Pemican and buffalo marrow,
Haunch of deer and hump of bison,
Yellow cakes of the Mondamin,
And the wild rice of the river.
But the gracious Hiawatha,
And the lovely Laughing Water,
And the careful old Nokomis,
Tasted not the food before them,
Only waited on the others,
Only served their guests in silence.
And when all the guests had finished,
Old Nokomis, brisk and busy,
From an ample pouch of otter,
Filled the red-stone pipes for smoking
With tobacco from the South-land,
Mixed with bark of the red willow,
And with herbs and leaves of fragrance.
Then she said, "O Pau-Puk-Keewis,
Dance for us your merry dances,
Dance the Beggar's Dance to please us,
That the feast may be more joyous,
That the time may pass more gayly,
And our guests be more contented!"
Then the handsome Pau-Puk-Keewis,
He the idle Yenadizze,
He the merry mischief-maker,
Whom the people called the Storm-Fool,
Rose among the guests assembled.

Skilled was he in sports and pastimes,
In the merry dance of snow-shoes,
In the play of quoits and ball-play;
Skilled was he in games of hazard,
In all games of skill and hazard,
Pugasaing, the Bowl and Counters,
Kuntassoo, the Game of Plum-stones.
Though the warriors called him Faint-Heart,
Called him coward, Shaugodaya,
Idler, gambler, Yenadizze,
Little heeded he their jesting,
Little cared he for their insults,
For the women and the maidens
Loved the handsome Pau-Puk-Keewis.
He was dressed in shirt of doeskin,
White and soft, and fringed with ermine,
All inwrought with beads of wampum;
He was dressed in deer-skin leggings,
Fringed with hedgehog quills and ermine,
And in moccasins of buck-skin,
Thick with quills and beads embroidered.
On his head were plumes of swan's down,
On his heels were tails of foxes,
In one hand a fan of feathers,

HE BEGAN HIS MYSTIC DANCES—*Page 204*

And a pipe was in the other.
Barred with streaks of red and yellow,
Streaks of blue and bright vermilion,
Shone the face of Pau-Puk-Keewis.
From his forehead fell his tresses,
Smooth, and parted like a woman's,
Shining bright with oil, and plaited,
Hung with braids of scented grasses,
As among the guests assembled,
To the sound of flutes and singing,
To the sound of drums and voices,
Rose the handsome Pau-Puk-Keewis,
And began his mystic dances.
First he danced a solemn measure,
Very slow in step and gesture,
In and out among the pine-trees,
Through the shadows and the sunshine,
Treading softly like a panther.
Then more swiftly and still swifter,
Whirling, spinning round in circles,
Leaping o'er the guests assembled,
Eddying round and round the wigwam,
Till the leaves went whirling with him,
Till the dust and wind together

Swept in eddies round about him.
Then along the sandy margin
Of the lake, the Big-Sea-Water,
On he sped with frenzied gestures,
Stamped upon the sand, and tossed it
Wildly in the air around him;
Till the wind became a whirlwind,
Till the sand was blown and sifted
Like great snowdrifts o'er the landscape,
Heaping all the shores with Sand Dunes,
Sand Hills of the Nagow Wudjoo!
Thus the merry Pau-Puk-Keewis
Danced his Beggar's Dance to please them,
And, returning, sat down laughing
There among the guests assembled,
Sat and fanned himself serenely
With his fan of turkey-feathers.
Then they said to Chibiabos,
To the friend of Hiawatha,
To the sweetest of all singers,
To the best of all musicians,
"Sing to us, O Chibiabos!
Songs of love and songs of longing,
That the feast may be more joyous,
That the time may pass more gayly,
And our guests be more contented!"
And the gentle Chibiabos
Sang in accents sweet and tender,
Sang in tones of deep emotion,
Songs of love and songs of longing;
Looking still at Hiawatha,
Looking at fair Laughing Water,
Sang he softly, sang in this wise:
"Onaway! Awake, beloved!
Thou the wild-flower of the forest!
Thou the wild-bird of the prairie!
Thou with eyes so soft and fawn-like!
"If thou only lookest at me,
I am happy, I am happy,
As the lilies of the prairie,
When they feel the dew upon them!
"Sweet thy breath is as the fragrance
Of the wild-flowers in the morning,
As their fragrance is at evening,
In the Moon when leaves are falling.
"Does not all the blood within me
Leap to meet thee, leap to meet thee,
As the springs to meet the sunshine,
In the Moon when nights are brightest?
"Onaway! my heart sings to thee,
Sings with joy when thou art near me,
As the sighing, singing branches
In the pleasant Moon of Strawberries!
"When thou art not pleased, beloved,
Then my heart is sad and darkened,
As the shining river darkens

When the clouds drop shadows on it.
"When thou smilest, my beloved,
Then my troubled heart is brightened,
As in sunshine gleam the ripples
That the cold wind makes in rivers.
"Smiles the earth, and smile the waters,
Smile the cloudless skies above us,
But I lose the way of smiling
When thou art no longer near me!
"I myself, myself! behold me!
Blood of my beating heart, behold me!
O awake, awake, beloved!
Onaway! awake, beloved!"
Thus the gentle Chibiabos
Sang his song of love and longing
And Iagoo, the great boaster,
He the marvelous story-teller,
He the friend of old Nokomis,
Jealous of the sweet musician,
Jealous of the applause they gave him,
Saw in all the eyes around him,
Saw in all their looks and gestures,
That the wedding guests assembled
Longed to hear his pleasant stories,
His immeasurable falsehoods.
Very boastful was Iagoo;
Never heard he an adventure
But himself had met a greater;
Never any deed of daring
But himself had done a bolder;
Never any marvelous story
But himself could tell a stranger.
Would you listen to his boasting,
Would you only give him credence,
No one ever shot an arrow
Half so far and high as he had;
Ever caught so many fishes,
Ever killed so many reindeer,
Ever trapped so many beavers!
None could run so fast as he could,
None could dive so deep as he could,
None could swim so far as he could;
None had made so many journeys,
None had seen so many wonders,
As this wonderful Iagoo,
As this marvelous story-teller!
Thus his name became a by-word
And a jest among the people;
And whene'er a boastful hunter
Praised his own address too highly,
Or a warrior, home returning,
Talked too much of his achievements,
All his hearers cried, "Iagoo!
Here's Iagoo come among us!"
He it was who carved the cradle
Of the little Hiawatha,

Carved its framework out of linden,
Bound it strong with reindeer sinew;
He it was who taught him later
How to make his bows and arrows,
How to make the bows of ash-tree,
And the arrows of the oak-tree.
So among the guests assembled
At my Hiawatha's wedding
Sat Iagoo, old and ugly,
Sat the marvelous story-teller.
And they said, "O good Iagoo,
Tell us now a tale of wonder,
Tell us of some strange adventure,
That the feast may be more joyous,
That the time may pass more gayly,
And our guests be more contented!"
And Iagoo answered straightway,
"You shall hear a tale of wonder.
You shall hear the strange adventures
Of Osseo, the Magician,
From the Evening Star descended."

XII

THE SON OF THE EVENING STAR

CAN it be the sun descending
O'er the level plain of water?
Or the Red Swan floating, flying,
Wounded by the magic arrow,
Staining all the waves with crimson,
With the crimson of its life-blood,
Filling all the air with splendor,
With the splendor of its plumage?
Yes; it is the sun descending,
Sinking down into the water;
All the sky is stained with purple,
All the water flushed with crimson!
No; it is the Red Swan floating,
Diving down beneath the water;
To the sky its wings are lifted,
With its blood the waves are reddened!
Over it the Star of Evening
Melts and trembles through the purple,
Hangs suspended in the twilight.
No; it is a bead of wampum
On the robes of the Great Spirit,
As he passes through the twilight,
Walks in silence through the heavens.
This with joy beheld Iagoo
And he said in haste: "Behold it!
See the sacred Star of Evening!
You shall hear a tale of wonder,
Hear the story of Osseo,

Son of the Evening Star, Osseo!
"Once, in days no more remembered,
Ages nearer the beginning,
When the heavens were closer to us,
And the Gods were more familiar,
In the North-land lived a hunter,
With ten young and comely daughters,
Tall and lithe as wands of willow;
Only Oweenee, the youngest,
She the willful and the wayward,
She the silent, dreamy maiden,
Was the fairest of the sisters.
"All these women married warriors,
Married brave and haughty husbands;
Only Oweenee, the youngest,
Laughed and flouted all her lovers,
All her young and handsome suitors,
And then married old Osseo,
Old Osseo, poor and ugly,
Broken with age and weak with coughing,
Always coughing like a squirrel.
"Ah, but beautiful within him
Was the Spirit of Osseo,
From the Evening Star descended,
Star of Evening, Star of Woman,
Star of tenderness and passion!
All its fire was in his bosom,
All its beauty in his spirit,
All its mystery in his being,
All its splendor in his language!
"And her lovers, the rejected,
Handsome men with belts of wampum,
Handsome men with paint and feathers,
Pointed at her in derision,
Followed her with jest and laughter.
But she said: 'I care not for you,
Care not for your belts of wampum,
Care not for your paint and feathers,
I am happy with Osseo!'
"Once to some great feast invited,
Through the damp and dusk of evening
Walked together the ten sisters,
Walked together with their husbands;
Slowly followed old Osseo,
With fair Oweenee beside him;
All the others chatted gayly,
These two only walked in silence.
"At the western sky Osseo
Gazed intent, as if imploring,
Often stopped and gazed imploring
At the trembling Star of Evening,
At the tender Star of Woman;
And they heard him murmur softly,
'Ah, showain nemeshin, Nosa!
Pity, pity me, my father!'
"'Listen!' said the eldest sister,

'He is praying to his father!
What a pity that the old man
Does not stumble in the pathway,
Does not break his neck by falling!'
And they laughed till all the forest
Rang with their unseemly laughter.
"On their pathway through the woodlands
Lay an oak, by storms uprooted,
Lay the great trunk of an oak-tree,
Buried half in leaves and mosses,
Mouldering, crumbling, huge and hollow,
And Osseo when he saw it,
Gave a shout, a cry of anguish,
Leaped into its yawning cavern,
At one end went in an old man,
Wasted, wrinkled, old, and ugly;
From the other came a young man,
Tall and straight and strong and handsome.
"Thus Osseo was transfigured,
Thus restored to youth and beauty;
But alas for good Osseo,
And for Oweenee, the faithful!
Strangely, too, was she transfigured.
Changed into a weak old woman,
With a staff she tottered onward,
Wasted, wrinkled, old, and ugly!
And the sisters and their husbands
Laughed until the echoing forest
Rang with their unseemly laughter.
"But Osseo turned not from her,
Walked with slower step beside her,
Took her hand, as brown and withered
As an oak-leaf is in Winter,
Called her sweetheart, Nenemoosha,
Soothed her with soft words of kindness,
Till they reached the lodge of feasting,
Till they sat down in the wigwam,
Sacred to the Star of Evening,
To the tender Star of Woman.
"Wrapt in visions, lost in dreaming,
At the banquet sat Osseo;
All were merry, all were happy,
All were joyous but Osseo,
Neither food nor drink he tasted,
Neither did he speak nor listen,
But as one bewildered sat he,
Looking dreamily and sadly,
First at Oweenee, then upward
At the gleaming sky above them.
"Then a voice was heard, a whisper.
Coming from the starry distance,
Coming from the empty vastness,
Low, and musical and tender;
And the voice said: 'O Osseo!
O my son, my best beloved!
Broken are the spells that bound you,

All the charms of the magicians,
All the magic powers of evil;
Come to me; ascend, Osseo!
"'Taste the food that stands before you;
It is blessed and enchanted,
It has magic virtues in it,
It will change you to a spirit.
All your bowls and all your kettles
Shall be wood and clay no longer;
But the bowls be changed to wampum,
And the kettles shall be silver;
They shall shine like shells of scarlet,
Like the fire shall gleam and glimmer.
"'And the women shall no longer
Bear the dreary doom of labor,
But be changed to birds, and glisten
With the beauty of the starlight,
Painted with the dusky splendors
Of the skies and clouds of evening!'
"What Osseo heard as whispers,
What as words he comprehended,
Was but music to the others,
Music as of birds afar off,
Of the whippoorwill afar off,
Of the lonely Wawonaissa
Singing in the darksome forest.
"Then the lodge began to tremble,
Straight began to shake and tremble,
And they felt it rising, rising,
Slowly through the air ascending,
From the darkness of the tree-tops
Forth into the dewy starlight,
Till it passed the topmost branches;
And behold! the wooden dishes
All were changed to shells of scarlet!
And behold! the earthen kettles
All were changed to bowls of silver!
And the roof-poles of the wigwam
Were as glittering rods of silver,
And the roof of bark upon them
As the shining shards of beetles.
"Then Osseo gazed around him,
And he saw the nine fair sisters,
All the sisters and their husbands,
Changed to birds of various plumage.
Some were jays and some were magpies,
Others thrushes, others blackbirds;
And they hopped, and sang, and twittered,
Pecked and fluttered all their feathers,
Strutted in their shining plumage,
And their tails like fans unfolded.
"Only Oweenee, the youngest,
Was not changed, but sat in silence,
Wasted, wrinkled, old, and ugly,
Looking sadly at the others;
Till Osseo, gazing upward,

Gave another cry of anguish,
Such a cry as he had uttered
By the oak-tree in the forest.
"Then returned her youth and beauty,
And her soiled and tattered garments
Were transformed to robes of ermine,
And her staff became a feather,
Yes, a shining silver feather!
"And again the wigwam trembled,
Swayed and rushed through airy currents,
Through transparent cloud and vapor,
And amid celestial splendors
On the Evening Star alighted,
As a snow-flake falls on snow-flake,
As a leaf drops on a river,
As the thistle-down on water.
"Forth with cheerful words of welcome
Came the father of Osseo,
He with radiant locks of silver,
He with eyes serene and tender.
And he said: 'My son, Osseo,
Hang the cage of birds you bring there,
Hang the cage with rods of silver,
And the birds with glistening feathers,
At the doorway of my wigwam.'
"At the door he hung the bird-cage,
And they entered in and gladly
Listened to Osseo's father,
Ruler of the Star of Evening,
As he said: 'O my Osseo!
I have had compassion on you,
Given you back your youth and beauty,
Into birds of various plumage
Changed your sisters and their husbands;
Changed them thus because they mocked you
In the figure of the old man,
In that aspect sad and wrinkled,
Could not see your heart of passion,
Could not see your youth immortal;
Only Oweenee, the faithful,
Saw your naked heart and loved you.
"'In the lodge that glimmers yonder,
In the little star that twinkles
Through the vapors, on the left hand,
Lives the envious Evil Spirit,
The Wabeno, the magician,
Who transformed you to an old man.
Take heed lest his beams fall on you,
For the rays he darts around him
Are the power of his enchantment,
Are the arrows that he uses.'
"Many years, in peace and quiet,
On the peaceful Star of Evening
Dwelt Osseo with his father;
Many years, in song and flutter,
At the doorway of the wigwam,

Hung the cage with rods of silver,
And fair Oweenee, the faithful,
Bore a son unto Osseo,
With the beauty of his mother,
With the courage of his father.
"And the boy grew up and prospered,
And Osseo, to delight him,
Made him little bows and arrows,
Opened the great cage of silver,
And let loose his aunts and uncles,
All those birds with glossy feathers
For his little son to shoot at.
"Round and round they wheeled and darted,
Filled the Evening Star with music,
With their songs of joy and freedom;
Filled the Evening Star with splendor,
With the fluttering of their plumage;
Till the boy, the little hunter,
Bent his bow and shot an arrow,
Shot a swift and fatal arrow,
And a bird, with shining feathers,
At his feet fell wounded sorely.
"But, O wondrous transformation!
'Twas no bird he saw before him,
'Twas a beautiful young woman,
With the arrow in her bosom!
"When her blood fell on the planet,
On the sacred Star of Evening,
Broken was the spell of magic,
Powerless was the strange enchantment,
And the youth, the fearless bowman,
Suddenly felt himself descending,
Held by unseen hands, but sinking
Downward through the empty spaces,
Downward through the clouds and vapors,
Till he rested on an island,
On an island, green and grassy,
Yonder in the Big-Sea-Water.
"After him he saw descending
All the birds with shining feathers,
Fluttering, falling, wafted downward,
Like the painted leaves of Autumn;
And the lodge with poles of silver,
With its roof like wings of beetles,
Like the shining shards of beetles,
By the winds of heaven uplifted,
Slowly sank upon the island,
Bringing back the good Osseo,
Bringing Oweenee, the faithful.

HE WAS HELD BY UNSEEN HANDS, BUT SINKING—

Page 221

"Then the birds, again transfigured,
Reassumed the shape of mortals,
Took their shape, but not their stature;
They remained as Little People,
Like the pygmies, the Puk-Wudjies,
And on pleasant nights of Summer,
When the Evening Star was shining,
Hand in hand they danced together,
On the island's craggy headlands,
On the sand-beach low and level.
"Still their glittering lodge is seen there,
On the tranquil Summer evenings,
And upon the shore the fisher
Sometimes hears their happy voices,
Sees them dancing in the starlight!"
When the story was completed,
When the wondrous tale was ended,
Looking round upon his listeners,
Solemnly Iagoo added:
"There are great men, I have known such,
Whom their people understand not,
Whom they even make a jest of,
Scoff and jeer at in derision.

87

From the story of Osseo
Let them learn the fate of jesters!"
All the wedding guests delighted
Listened to the marvelous story,
Listened laughing and applauding,
And they whispered to each other:
"Does he mean himself, I wonder?
And are we the aunts and uncles?"
Then again sang Chibiabos,
Sang a song of love and longing,
In those accents sweet and tender,
In those tones of pensive sadness,
Sang a maiden's lamentation
For her lover, her Algonquin.
"When I think of my beloved,
Ah me! think of my beloved,
When my heart is thinking of him,
O my sweetheart, my Algonquin!
"Ah me! when I parted from him,
Round my neck he hung the wampum,
As a pledge, the snow-white wampum,
O my sweetheart, my Algonquin!
"I will go with you, he whispered,
Ah me! to your native country;
Let me go with you, he whispered,
O my sweetheart, my Algonquin!
"Far away, away, I answered,
Very far away, I answered,
Ah me! is my native country,
O my sweetheart, my Algonquin!
"When I looked back to behold him,
Where we parted, to behold him,
After me he still was gazing,
O my sweetheart, my Algonquin!
"By the tree he still was standing,
By the fallen tree was standing,
That had dropped into the water,
O my sweetheart, my Algonquin!
"When I think of my beloved,
Ah me! think of my beloved,
When my heart is thinking of him,
O my sweetheart, my Algonquin!"
Such was Hiawatha's Wedding,
Such the dance of Pau-Puk-Keewis,
Such the story of Iagoo,
Such the songs of Chibiabos;
Thus the wedding banquet ended,
And the wedding guests departed,
Leaving Hiawatha happy
With the night and Minnehaha.

XIII

BLESSING THE CORNFIELDS

SING, O song of Hiawatha,
Of the happy days that followed,
In the land of the Ojibways,
In the pleasant land and peaceful!
Sing the mysteries of Mondamin,
Sing the Blessings of the Cornfields!
Buried was the bloody hatchet,
Buried was the dreadful war-club,
Buried were all warlike weapons,
And the war-cry was forgotten.
There was peace among the nations;
Unmolested roved the hunters,
Built the birch canoe for sailing,
Caught the fish in lake and river,
Shot the deer and trapped the beaver,
Unmolested worked the women,
Made their sugar from the maple,
Gathered wild rice in the meadows,
Dressed the skins of deer and beaver.
All around the happy village
Stood the maize-fields, green and shining,
Waved the green plumes of Mondamin,
Waved his soft and sunny tresses,
Filling all the land with plenty.
'Twas the women who in Springtime,
Planted the broad fields and fruitful,
Buried in the earth Mondamin;
'Twas the women who in Autumn
Stripped the yellow husks of harvest,
Stripped the garments from Mondamin,
Even as Hiawatha taught them.
Once, when all the maize was planted,
Hiawatha, wise and thoughtful,
Spake and said to Minnehaha,
To his wife, the Laughing Water:
"You shall bless to-night the cornfields,
Draw a magic circle round them,
To protect them from destruction,
Blast of mildew, blight of insect,
Wagemin, the thief of cornfields,
Paimosaid, who steals the maize-ear!
"In the night, when all is silence,
In the night when all is darkness,
When the Spirit of Sleep, Nepahwin,
Shuts the doors of all the wigwams,
So that not an ear can hear you,
So that not an eye can see you,
Rise up from your bed in silence,
Lay aside your garments wholly,
Walk around the fields you planted,
Round the borders of the cornfields,
Covered by your tresses only,
Robed with darkness as a garment.
"Thus the fields shall be more fruitful,

And the passing of your footsteps
Draw a magic circle round them,
So that neither blight nor mildew,
Neither burrowing worm nor insect,
Shall pass o'er the magic circle;
Not the dragon-fly, Kwo-ne-she,
Nor the spider, Subbekashe,
Nor the grasshopper, Pah-puk-keena
Nor the mighty caterpillar,
Way-muk-kwana, with the bearskin,
King of all the caterpillars!"
On the tree-tops near the cornfields
Sat the hungry crows and ravens,
Kahgahgee, the King of Ravens,
With his band of black marauders,
And they laughed at Hiawatha,
Till the tree-tops shook with laughter,
With their melancholy laughter,
At the words of Hiawatha,
"Hear him!" said they; "hear the Wise Man,
Hear the plots of Hiawatha!"
When the noiseless night descended
Broad and dark o'er field and forest,
When the mournful Wawonaissa,
Sorrowing sang among the hemlocks,
And the Spirit of Sleep, Nepahwin,
Shut the doors of all the wigwams,
From her bed rose Laughing Water,
Laid aside her garments wholly,
And with darkness clothed and guarded,
Unashamed and unaffrighted,
Walked securely round the cornfields,
Drew the sacred, magic circle
Of her footprints round the cornfields.
No one but the Midnight only
Saw her beauty in the darkness,
No one but the Wawonaissa
Heard the panting of her bosom;
Guskewau, the darkness, wrapped her
Closely in his sacred mantle,
So that none might see her beauty,
So that none might boast, "I saw her!"
On the morrow, as the day dawned,
Kahgahgee, the King of Ravens,
Gathered all his black marauders,
Crows and blackbirds, jays, and ravens,
Clamorous on the dusky tree-tops,
And descended, fast and fearless,
On the fields of Hiawatha,
On the grave of the Mondamin.
"We will drag Mondamin," said they,
"From the grave where he is buried,
Spite of all the magic circles
Laughing Water draws around it,
Spite of all the sacred footprints
Minnehaha stamps upon it!"

But the wary Hiawatha,
Ever thoughtful, careful, watchful,
Had o'erheard the scornful laughter
When they mocked him from the tree-tops.
"Kaw!" he said, "my friends the ravens!
Kahgahgee, my King of Ravens!
I will teach you all a lesson
That shall not be soon forgotten!"
He had risen before the daybreak,
He had spread o'er all the cornfields
Snares to catch the black marauders,
And was lying now in ambush
In the neighboring grove of pine-trees,
Waiting for the crows and blackbirds,
Waiting for the jays and ravens.
Soon they came with caw and clamor,
Rush of wings and cry of voices,
To their work of devastation,
Settling down upon the cornfields,
Delving deep with beak and talon,
For the body of Mondamin.
And with all their craft and cunning,
All their skill in wiles of warfare,
They perceived no danger near them,
Till their claws became entangled,
Till they found themselves imprisoned
In the snares of Hiawatha.
From his place of ambush came he,
Striding terrible among them,
And so awful was his aspect
That the bravest quailed with terror,
Without mercy he destroyed them
Right and left, by tens and twenties,
And their wretched, lifeless bodies
Hung aloft on poles for scarecrows
Round the consecrated cornfields,
As a signal of his vengeance,
As a warning to marauders.
Only Kahgahgee, the leader.
Kahgahgee, the King of Ravens,
He alone was spared among them
As a hostage for his people.
With his prisoner-string he bound him,
Led him captive to his wigwam,
Tied him fast with cords of elm-bark
To the ridge-pole of his wigwam.
"Kahgahgee, my raven!" said he,
"You the leader of the robbers,
You the plotter of this mischief,
The contriver of this outrage,
I will keep you, I will hold you,
As a hostage for your people,
As a pledge of good behavior!"
And he left him, grim and sulky,
Sitting in the morning sunshine
On the summit of the wigwam,

Croaking fiercely his displeasure,
Flapping his great sable pinions,
Vainly struggling for his freedom,
Vainly calling on his people!
Summer passed, and Shawondasee
Breathed his sighs o'er all the landscape,
From the South-land sent his ardors,
Wafted kisses warm and tender;
And the maize-field grew and ripened,
Till it stood in all the splendor
Of its garments green and yellow,
Of its tassels and its plumage,
And the maize-ears full and shining
Gleamed from bursting sheaths of verdure.
Then Nokomis, the old woman,
Spake, and said to Minnehaha:
"'Tis the Moon when leaves are falling;
All the wild-rice has been gathered,
And the maize is ripe and ready;
Let us gather in the harvest,
Let us wrestle with Mondamin,
Strip him of his plumes and tassels,
Of his garments green and yellow!"
And the merry Laughing Water
Went rejoicing from the wigwam,
With Nokomis, old and wrinkled,
And they called the women round them,
Called the young men and the maidens,
To the harvest of the cornfields,
To the husking of the maize-ear.
On the border of the forest,
Underneath the fragrant pine-trees,
Sat the old men and the warriors
Smoking in the pleasant shadow.
In uninterrupted silence
Looked they at the gamesome labor
Of the young men and the women;
Listened to their noisy talking,
To their laughter and their singing,
Heard them chattering like the magpies,
Heard them laughing like the blue-jays,
Heard them singing like the robins.
And whene'er some lucky maiden
Found a red ear in the husking,
Found a maize-ear red as blood is,
"Nushka!" cried they all together,
"Nushka! you shall have a sweetheart,
You shall have a handsome husband!"
"Ugh!" the old men all responded
From their seats beneath the pine-trees.
And whene'er a youth or maiden
Found a crooked ear in husking,
Found a maize-ear in the husking,
Blighted, mildewed, or misshapen,
Then they laughed and sang together,
Crept and limped about the cornfields

Mimicked in their gait and gestures
Some old man, bent almost double,
Singing singly or together:
"Wagemin, the thief of cornfields!
Paimosaid, the skulking robber!"
Till the cornfields rang with laughter,
Till from Hiawatha's wigwam
Kahgahgee, the King of Ravens,
Screamed and quivered in his anger,
And from all the neighboring tree-tops
Cawed and croaked the black marauders.
"Ugh!" the old men all responded,
From their seats beneath the pine-trees!

XIV

PICTURE-WRITING

IN those days said Hiawatha,
"Lo! how all things fade and perish!
From the memory of the old men
Fade away the great traditions,
The achievements of the warriors,
The adventures of the hunters,
All the wisdom of the Medas,
All the craft of the Wabenos,
All the marvelous dreams and visions
Of the Jossakeeds, the Prophets!
"Great men die and are forgotten,
Wise men speak; their words of wisdom
Perish in the ears that hear them,
Do not reach the generations
That, as yet unborn, are waiting
In the great, mysterious darkness
Of the speechless days that shall be!
"On the grave-posts of our fathers
Are no signs, no figures painted;
Who are in those graves we know not,
Only know they are our fathers.
Of what kith they are and kindred,
From what old, ancestral Totem,
Be it Eagle, Bear, or Beaver,
They descended, this we know not,
Only know they are our fathers.
"Face to face we speak together,
But we cannot speak when absent,
Cannot send our voices from us
To the friends that dwell afar off;
Cannot send a secret message,
But the bearer learns our secret,
May pervert it, may betray it,
May reveal it unto others."
Thus said Hiawatha, walking
In the solitary forest,

Pondering, musing in the forest,
On the welfare of his people.
From his pouch he took his colors,
Took his paints of different colors,
On the smooth bark of a birch-tree
Painted many shapes and figures,
Wonderful and mystic figures,

"AND EACH FIGURE HAD A MEANING"—*Page 236*

   And each figure had a meaning,
Each some word or thought suggested.
Gitche Manito the Mighty,
He, the Master of Life, was painted
As an egg, with points projecting
To the four winds of the heavens.
Everywhere is the Great Spirit,
Was the meaning of this symbol.
Mitche Manito the Mighty,
He the dreadful Spirit of Evil,
As a serpent was depicted,
As Kenabeek, the great serpent.
Very crafty, very cunning,
Is the creeping Spirit of Evil,
Was the meaning of this symbol.

94

Life and Death he drew as circles,
Life was white, but Death was darkened;
Sun and moon and stars he painted,
Man and beast, and fish and reptile,
Forests, mountains, lakes, and rivers.
For the earth he drew a straight line,
For the sky a bow above it;
White the space between for day-time,
Filled with little stars for night-time;
On the left a point for sunrise,
On the right a point for sunset,
On the top a point for noontide,
And for rain and cloudy weather
Waving lines descending from it.
Footprints pointing towards a wigwam
Were a sign of invitation,
Were a sign of guests assembling:
Bloody hands with palms uplifted
Were a symbol of destruction,
Were a hostile sign and symbol.
All these things did Hiawatha
Show unto his wondering people,
And interpreted their meaning,
And he said: "Behold, your graveposts
Have no mark, no sign, nor symbol.
Go and paint them all with figures;
Each one with its household symbol,
With its own ancestral Totem,
So that those who follow after
May distinguish them and know them."
And they painted on the graveposts
Of the graves yet unforgotten,
Each his own ancestral Totem,
Each the symbol of his household;
Figures of the Bear and Reindeer,
Of the Turtle, Crane, and Beaver,
Each inverted as a token
That the owner was departed,
That the chief who bore the symbol
Lay beneath in dust and ashes.
And the Jossakeeds, the Prophets,
The Wabenos, the Magicians,
And the Medicine-men, the Medas,
Painted upon bark and deer-skin
Figures for the songs they chanted,
For each song a separate symbol,
Figures mystical and awful,
Figures strange and brightly colored;
And each figure had its meaning,
Each some magic song suggested.
The Great Spirit, the Creator,
Flashing light through all the heaven;
The Great Serpent, the Kenabeek,
With his bloody crest erected,
Creeping, looking into heaven;
In the sky the sun, that listens,

And the moon eclipsed and dying;
Owl and eagle, crane and hen-hawk,
And the cormorant, bird of magic;
Headless men, that walk the heavens,
Bodies lying pierced with arrows,
Bloody hands of death uplifted,
Flags on graves, and great war-captains
Grasping both the earth and heaven!
Such as these the shapes they painted
On the birch-bark and the deer-skin;
Songs of war and songs of hunting,
Songs of medicine and of magic,
All were written in these figures,
For each figure had its meaning,
Each its separate song recorded.
Nor forgotten was the Love-Song,
The most subtle of all medicines,
The most potent spell of magic,
Dangerous more than war or hunting!
Thus the Love-Song was recorded,
Symbol and interpretation.
First a human figure standing,
Painted in the brightest scarlet;
'Tis the lover, the musician,
And the meaning is, "My painting
Makes me powerful over others."
Then the figure seated, singing,
Playing on a drum of magic,
And the interpretation, "Listen!
'Tis my voice you hear, my singing!"
Then the same red figure seated
In the shelter of a wigwam,
And the meaning of the symbol,
"I will come and sit beside you
In the mystery of my passion!"
Then two figures, man and woman,
Standing hand in hand together
With their hands so clasped together
That they seem in one united,
And the words thus represented
Are, "I see your heart within you,
And your cheeks are red with blushes!"
Next the maiden on an island,
In the centre of an island;
And the song this shape suggested
Was, "Though you were at a distance,
Were upon some far-off island,
Such the spell I cast upon you,
Such the magic power of passion,
I could straightway draw you to me!"
Then the figure of the maiden
Sleeping, and the lover near her,
Whispering to her in her slumbers,
Saying, "Though you were far from me
In the land of Sleep and Silence,
Still the voice of love would reach you!"

And the last of all the figures
Was a heart within a circle,
Drawn within a magic circle;
And the image had this meaning:
"Naked lies your heart before me,
To your naked heart I whisper!"
Thus it was that Hiawatha,
In his wisdom, taught the people
All the mysteries of painting,
All the art of Picture-Writing,
On the smooth bark of the birch-tree,
On the white skin of the reindeer,
On the grave-posts of the village.

XV

HIAWATHA'S LAMENTATION

IN those days the Evil Spirits,
All the Manitos of mischief,
Fearing Hiawatha's wisdom,
And his love for Chibiabos,
Jealous of their faithful friendship,
And their noble words and actions,
Made at length a league against them,
To molest them and destroy them.
Hiawatha, wise and wary,
Often said to Chibiabos,
"O my brother! do not leave me,
Lest the Evil Spirits harm you!"
Chibiabos, young and heedless,
Laughing shook his coal-black tresses,
Answered ever sweet and childlike,
"Do not fear for me, O brother!
Harm and evil come not near me!"
Once when Peboan, the Winter,
Roofed with ice the Big-Sea-Water,
When the snow-flakes, whirling downward,
Hissed among the withered oak-leaves,
Changed the pine-trees into wigwams,
Covered all the earth with silence,—
Armed with arrows, shod with snow-shoes,
Heeding not his brother's warning,
Fearing not the Evil Spirits,
Forth to hunt the deer with antlers
All alone went Chibiabos.
Right across the Big-Sea-Water
Sprang with speed the deer before him.
With the wind and snow he followed,
O'er the treacherous ice he followed,
Wild with all the fierce commotion
And the rapture of the hunting.
But beneath, the Evil Spirits
Lay in ambush, waiting for him,

Broke the treacherous ice beneath him,
Dragged him downward to the bottom,
Buried in the sand his body,
Unktahee, the god of water,
He, the god of the Dacotahs,
Drowned him in the deep abysses
Of the lake of Gitche Gumee.
From the headlands Hiawatha
Sent forth such a wail of anguish,
Such a fearful lamentation,
That the bison paused to listen,
And the wolves howled from the prairies,
And the thunder in the distance
Woke and answered "Baim-wawa!"
Then his face with black he painted,
With his robe his head he covered,
In his wigwam sat lamenting,
Seven long weeks he sat lamenting,
Uttering still this moan of sorrow:—
"He is dead, the sweet musician!
He, the sweetest of all singers!
He has gone from us forever,
He has moved a little nearer
To the Master of all music,
To the Master of all singing!
O my brother, Chibiabos!"
And the melancholy fir-trees
Waved their dark green fans above him,
Waved their purple cones above him,
Sighing with him to console him,
Mingling with his lamentation
Their complaining, their lamenting.
Came the Spring, and all the forest
Looked in vain for Chibiabos;
Sighed the rivulet, Sebowisha,
Sighed the rushes in the meadow.
From the tree-tops sang the bluebird,
Sang the bluebird, the Owaissa,
"Chibiabos! Chibiabos!
He is dead, the sweet musician!"
From the wigwam sang the robin,
Sang the Opechee, the robin,
"Chibiabos! Chibiabos!
He is dead, the sweetest singer!"
And at night, through all the forest
Went the whippoorwill complaining,
Wailing went the Wawonaissa,
"Chibiabos! Chibiabos!
He is dead, the sweet musician!
He the sweetest of all singers!"
Then the medicine-men, the Medas,
The magicians, the Wabenos,
And the Jossakeeds, the prophets,
Came to visit Hiawatha;
Built a Sacred Lodge beside him,
To appease him, to console him,

98

Walked in silent, grave procession,
Bearing each a pouch of healing,
Skin of beaver, lynx, or otter,
Filled with magic roots and simples,
Filled with very potent medicines.
When he heard their steps approaching,
Hiawatha ceased lamenting,
Called no more on Chibiabos;
Naught he questioned, naught he answered,
But his mournful head uncovered,
From his face the mourning colors
Washed he slowly and in silence,
Slowly and in silence followed
Onward to the Sacred Wigwam.
There a magic drink they gave him,
Made of Nahma-wusk, the spearmint,
And Wabeno-wusk, the yarrow,
Roots of power, and herbs of healing;
Beat their drums, and shook their rattles;
Chanted singly and in chorus,
Mystic songs like these, they chanted.
"I myself, myself! behold me!
'Tis the great Gray Eagle talking;
Come, ye white crows, come and hear him!
The loud-speaking thunder helps me;
All the unseen spirits help me;
I can hear their voices calling,
All around the sky I hear them!
I can blow you strong, my brother,
I can heal you, Hiawatha!"
"Hi-au-ha!" replied the chorus,
"Way-ha-way!" the mystic chorus.
"Friends of mine are all the serpents!
Hear me shake my skin of hen-hawk!
Mahng, the white loon, I can kill him;
I can shoot your heart and kill it!
I can blow you strong, my brother,
I can heal you, Hiawatha!"
"Hi-au-ha!" replied the chorus,
"Way-ha-way!" the mystic chorus.
"I myself, myself! the prophet!
When I speak the wigwam trembles,
Shakes the Sacred Lodge with terror,
Hands unseen begin to shake it!
When I walk, the sky I tread on
Bends and makes a noise beneath me!
I can blow you strong, my brother!
Rise and speak, O Hiawatha!"
"Hi-au-ha!" replied the chorus,
"Way-ha-way!" the mystic chorus.
Then they shook their medicine-pouches
O'er the head of Hiawatha,
Danced their medicine-dance around him;
And upstarting wild and haggard,
Like a man from dreams awakened,
He was healed of all his madness.

As the clouds are swept from heaven,
Straightway from his brain departed
All his moody melancholy;
As the ice is swept from rivers,
Straightway from his heart departed
All his sorrow and affliction.
Then they summoned Chibiabos
From his grave beneath the waters,
From the sands of Gitche Gumee
Summoned Hiawatha's brother.
And so mighty was the magic
Of that cry and invocation,
That he heard it as he lay there
Underneath the Big-Sea-Water;
From the sand he rose and listened,
Heard the music and the singing,
Came, obedient to the summons,
To the doorway of the wigwam,
But to enter they forbade him.
Through a chink a coal they gave him,
Through the door a burning fire-brand;
Ruler in the Land of Spirits,
Ruler o'er the dead, they made him,
Telling him a fire to kindle
For all those that died thereafter,
Camp-fires for their night encampments
On their solitary journey
To the kingdom of Ponemah,
To the land of the Hereafter.
From the village of his childhood,
From the homes of those who knew him,
Passing silent through the forest,
Like a smoke-wreath wafted sideways,
Slowly vanished Chibiabos!
Where he passed, the branches moved not,
Where he trod the grasses bent not,
And the fallen leaves of last year
Made no sound beneath his footsteps.
Four whole days he journeyed onward
Down the pathway of the dead men;
On the dead-man's strawberry feasted,
Crossed the melancholy river,
On the swinging log he crossed it,
Came unto the Lake of Silver.
In the Stone Canoe was carried
To the Islands of the Blessed,
To the land of ghosts and shadows.
On that journey, moving slowly,
Many weary spirits saw he,
Panting under heavy burdens,
Laden with war-clubs, bows and arrows,
Robes of fur, and pots and kettles,
And with food that friends had given
For that solitary journey.
"Aye! why do the living," said they,
"Lay such heavy burdens on us!

Better were it to go naked,
Better were it to go fasting,
Than to bear such heavy burdens
On our long and weary journey!"
Forth then issued Hiawatha,
Wandered eastward, wandered westward,
Teaching men the use of simples
And the antidotes for poisons,
And the cure of all diseases.
Thus was first made known to mortals
All the mystery of Medamin,
All the sacred art of healing.

XVI

PAU-PUK-KEEWIS

YOU shall hear how Pau-Puk-Keewis,
He, the handsome Yenadizze,
Whom the people called the Storm Fool,
Vexed the village with disturbance;
You shall hear of all his mischief,
And his flight from Hiawatha,
And his wondrous transmigrations,
And the end of his adventures.
On the shores of Gitche Gumee,
On the dunes of Nagow Wudjoo,
By the shining Big-Sea-Water
Stood the lodge of Pau-Puk-Keewis.
It was he who in his frenzy
Whirled these drifting sands together,
On the dunes of Nagow Wudjoo,
When, among the guests assembled,
He so merrily and madly
Danced at Hiawatha's wedding,
Danced the Beggars' Dance to please them.
Now, in search of new adventures,
From his lodge went Pau-Puk-Keewis,
Came with speed into the village,
Found the young men all assembled
In the lodge of old Iagoo,
Listening to his monstrous stories,
To his wonderful adventures.
He was telling them the story
Of Ojeeg, the Summer-Maker,
How he made a hole in heaven,
How he climbed up into heaven,
And let out the summer-weather,
The perpetual, pleasant Summer;
How the Otter first essayed it;
How the Beaver, Lynx, and Badger,
Tried in turn the great achievement,
From the summit of the mountain

Smote their fists against the heavens,
Smote against the sky their foreheads,
Cracked the sky, but could not break it,
How the Wolverine, uprising,
Made him ready for the encounter,
Bent his knees down, like a squirrel,
Drew his arms back, like a cricket.
"Once he leaped," said old Iagoo,
"Once he leaped, and lo! above him
Bent the sky, as ice in rivers
When the waters rise beneath it;
Twice he leaped, and lo! above him
Cracked the sky, as ice in rivers
When the freshet is at highest!
Thrice he leaped, and lo! above him
Broke the shattered sky asunder,
And he disappeared within it,
And Ojeeg, the Fisher Weasel,
With a bound went in behind him!"
"Hark you!" shouted Pau-Puk-Keewis
As he entered at the doorway;
"I am tired of all this talking,
Tired of old Iagoo's stories,
Tired of Hiawatha's wisdom.
Here is something to amuse you,
Better than this endless talking."
Then from out his pouch of wolf-skin
Forth he drew, with solemn manner,
All the game of Bowl and Counters,
Pugasaing, with thirteen pieces.
White on one side were they painted,
And vermilion on the other;
Two Kenabeeks or great serpents,
Two Ininewug or wedge-men,
One great war-club, Pugamaugun,
And one slender fish, the Keego,
Four round pieces, Ozawabeeks,
And three Sheshebwug or ducklings.
All were made of bone and painted,
All except the Ozawabeeks;
These were brass, on one side burnished,
And were black upon the other.
In a wooden bowl he placed them,
Shook and jostled them together,
Threw them on the ground before him.
Thus exclaiming and explaining:
"Red side up are all the pieces,
And one great Kenabeek standing
On the bright side of a brass piece,
On a burnished Ozawabeek;
Thirteen tens and eight are counted."
Then again he shook the pieces,
Shook and jostled them together,
Threw them on the ground before him,
Still exclaiming and explaining:
"White are both the great Kenabeeks,

White the Ininewug, the wedge-men,
Red are all the other pieces;
Five tens and an eight are counted."
Thus he taught the game of hazard,
Thus displayed it and explained it,
Running through its various chances,
Various changes, various meanings:
Twenty curious eyes stared at him,
Full of eagerness stared at him.
"Many games," said old Iagoo,
"Many games of skill and hazard
Have I seen in different nations,
Have I played in different countries.
He who plays with old Iagoo
Must have very nimble fingers;
Though you think yourself so skillful
I can beat you, Pau-Puk-Keewis,
I can even give you lessons
In your game of Bowl and Counters!"
So they sat and played together,
All the old men and the young men,
Played for dresses, weapons, wampum,
Played till midnight, played till morning,
Played until the Yenadizze,
Till the cunning Pau-Puk-Keewis,
Of their treasures had despoiled them,
Of the best of all their dresses,
Shirts of deer-skin, robes of ermine,
Belts of wampum, crests of feathers,
Warlike weapons, pipes and pouches.
Twenty eyes glared wildly at him,
Like the eyes of wolves glared at him.
Said the lucky Pau-Puk-Keewis:
"In my wigwam I am lonely,
In my wanderings and adventures
I have need of a companion,
Fain would have a Meshinauwa,
An attendant and pipe-bearer.
I will venture all these winnings,
All these garments heaped about me,
All this wampum, all these feathers,
On a single throw will venture
All against the young man yonder!"
'Twas a youth of sixteen summers,
'Twas a nephew of Iagoo;
Face-in-a-Mist, the people called him.
As the fire burns in a pipe-head
Dusky red beneath the ashes,
So beneath his shaggy eyebrows
Glowed the eyes of old Iagoo.
"Ugh!" he answered very fiercely:
"Ugh!" they answered all and each one.
Seized the wooden bowl the old man,
Closely in his bony fingers
Clutched the fatal bowl, Onagon,
Shook it fiercely and with fury,

Made the pieces ring together
As he threw them down before him.
Red were both the great Kenabeeks,
Red the Ininewug, the wedge-men,
Red the Sheshebwug, the ducklings,
Black the four brass Ozawabeeks,
White alone the fish, the Keego;
Only five the pieces counted!
Then the smiling Pau-Puk-Keewis
Shook the bowl and threw the pieces;
Lightly in the air he tossed them,
And they fell about him scattered;
Dark and bright the Ozawabeeks,
Red and white the other pieces,
And upright among the others
One Ininewug was standing,
Even as crafty Pau-Puk-Keewis
Stood alone among the players,
Saying, "Five tens! mine the game is!"
Twenty eyes glared at him fiercely,
Like the eyes of wolves glared at him,
As he turned and left the wigwam,
Followed by his Meshinauwa,
By the nephew of Iagoo,
By the tall and graceful stripling,
Bearing in his arms the winnings,
Shirts of deer-skin, robes of ermine,
Belts of wampum, pipes and weapons.
"Carry them," said Pau-Puk-Keewis,
Pointing with his fan of feathers,
"To my wigwam far to eastward,
On the dunes of Nagow Wudjoo!"
Hot and red with smoke and gambling
Were the eyes of Pau-Puk-Keewis
As he came forth to the freshness
Of the pleasant summer morning.
All the birds were singing gayly,
All the streamlets flowing swiftly,
And the heart of Pau-Puk-Keewis
Sang with pleasure as the birds sing,
Beat with triumph like the streamlets,
As he wandered through the village,
In the early gray of morning,
With his fan of turkey-feathers,
With his plumes and tufts of swan's down,
Till he reached the farthest wigwam,
Reached the lodge of Hiawatha.
Silent was it and deserted;
No one met him at the doorway,
No one came to bid him welcome.
But the birds were singing round it,
In and out and round the doorway,
Hopping, singing, fluttering, feeding,—
And aloft upon the ridge-pole
Kahgahgee, the King of Ravens,
Sat with fiery eyes, and, screaming,

Flapped his wings at Pau-Puk-Keewis,
"All are gone! the lodge is empty!"
Thus it was spake Pau-Puk-Keewis,
In his heart resolving mischief;
"Gone is wary Hiawatha,
Gone the silly Laughing Water,
Gone Nokomis, the old woman,
And the lodge is left unguarded!"
By the neck he seized the raven,
Whirled it round him like a rattle,
Like a medicine-pouch he shook it,
Strangled Kahgahgee, the raven,
From the ridge-pole of the wigwam
Left its lifeless body hanging,
As an insult to its master,
As a taunt to Hiawatha.
With a stealthy step he entered,
Round the lodge in wild disorder
Threw the household things about him,
Piled together in confusion
Bowls of wood and earthen kettles,
Robes of buffalo and beaver,
Skins of otter, lynx, and ermine,
As an insult to Nokomis,
As a taunt to Minnehaha.
Then departed Pau-Puk-Keewis,
Whistling, singing through the forest,
Whistling gayly to the squirrels,
Who from hollow boughs above him
Dropped their acorn-shells upon him,
Singing gayly to the wood birds,
Who from out the leafy darkness
Answered with a song as merry.
Then he climbed the rocky headlands,
Looking o'er the Gitche Gumee,
Perched himself upon their summit,
Waiting full of mirth and mischief
The return of Hiawatha.
Stretched upon his back he lay there;
Far below him plashed the waters,
Plashed and washed the dreamy waters;
Far above him swam the heavens,
Swam the dizzy, dreamy heavens;
Round him hovered, fluttered, rustled,
Hiawatha's mountain chickens,
Flock-wise swept and wheeled about him,
Almost brushed him with their pinions.
And he killed them as he lay there,
Slaughtered them by tens and twenties,
Threw their bodies down the headland,
Threw them on the beach below him,
Till at length Kayoshk, the sea-gull,
Perched upon a crag above them,
Shouted: "It is Pau-Puk-Keewis!
He is slaying us by hundreds!
Send a message to our brother,

Tidings send to Hiawatha!"

XVII

THE HUNTING OF PAU-PUK-KEEWIS

FULL of wrath was Hiawatha
When he came into the village,
Found the people in confusion,
Heard of all the misdemeanors,
All the malice and the mischief,
Of the cunning Pau-Puk-Keewis.
Hard his breath came through his nostrils,
Through his teeth he buzzed and muttered
Words of anger and resentment,
Hot and humming like a hornet,
"I will slay this Pau-Puk-Keewis,
Slay this mischief-maker!" said he.
"Not so long and wide the world is,
Not so rude and rough the way is,
That my wrath shall not attain him,
That my vengeance shall not reach him!"
Then in swift pursuit departed,
Hiawatha and the hunters
On the trail of Pau-Puk-Keewis,
Through the forest, where he passed it,
To the headlands where he rested;
But they found not Pau-Puk-Keewis,
Only in the trampled grasses,
In the whortleberry bushes,
Found the couch where he had rested,
Found the impress of his body.
From the lowlands far beneath them,
From the Muskoday, the meadow,
Pau-Puk-Keewis, turning backward,
Made a gesture of defiance,
Made a gesture of derision;
And aloud cried Hiawatha,
From the summit of the mountain:
"Not so long and wide the world is,
Not so rude and rough the way is,
But my wrath shall overtake you,
And my vengeance shall attain you!"
Over rock and over river,
Through bush, and break, and forest,
Ran the cunning Pau-Puk-Keewis;
Like an antelope he bounded,
Till he came into a streamlet
In the middle of the forest,
To a streamlet still and tranquil,
That had overflowed its margin,
To a dam made by the beavers,
To a pond of quiet waters,
Where knee-deep the trees were standing,

Where the water-lilies floated,
Where the rushes waved and whispered.
On the dam stood Pau-Puk-Keewis,
On the dam of trunks and branches,
Through whose chinks the water spouted,
O'er whose summit flowed the streamlet.
From the bottom rose the beaver,
Looked with two great eyes of wonder,
Eyes that seemed to ask a question,
At the stranger, Pau-Puk-Keewis.
On the dam stood Pau-Puk-Keewis,
O'er his ankles flowed the streamlet,
Flowed the bright and silvery water,
And he spake unto the beaver,
With a smile he spake in this wise:
"O my friend Ahmeek, the beaver,
Cool and pleasant is the water;
Let me dive into the water,
Let me rest there in your lodges;
Change me, too, into a beaver!"
Cautiously replied the beaver,
With reserve he thus made answer:
"Let me first consult the others,
Let me ask the other beavers."
Down he sank into the water,
Heavily sank he, as a stone sinks,
Down among the leaves and branches,
Brown and matted at the bottom.
On the dam stood Pau-Puk-Keewis,
O'er his ankles flowed the streamlet,
Spouted through the chinks below him,
Dashed upon the stones beneath him,
Spread serene and calm before him,
And the sunshine and the shadows
Fell in flecks and gleams upon him,
Fell in little shining patches,
Through the waving, rustling branches.
From the bottom rose the beavers,
Silently above the surface
Rose one head and then another,
Till the pond seemed full of beavers,
Full of black and shining faces.
To the beavers Pau-Puk-Keewis
Spake entreating, said in this wise:
"Very pleasant is your dwelling,
O my friends! and safe from danger;
Can you not with all your cunning,
All your wisdom and contrivance,
Change me, too, into a beaver?"
"Yes!" replied Ahmeek, the beaver,
He the King of all the beavers,
"Let yourself slide down among us,
Down into the tranquil water."
Down into the pond among them
Silently sank Pau-Puk-Keewis;
Black became his shirt of deer-skin,

Black his moccasins and leggings,
In a broad black tail behind him
Spread his fox-tail and his fringes;
He was changed into a beaver.
"Make me large," said Pau-Puk-Keewis,
"Make me large and make me larger,
Larger than the other beavers."
"Yes," the beaver chief responded,
"When our lodge below you enter,
In our wigwam we will make you
Ten times larger than the others."
Thus into the clear brown water
Silently sank Pau-Puk-Keewis;
Found the bottom covered over
With the trunks of trees and branches,
Hoards of food against the winter,
Piles and heaps against the famine;
Found the lodge with arching doorway,
Leading into spacious chambers.
Here they made him large and larger,
Made him largest of the beavers,
Ten times larger than the others.
"You shall be our ruler," said they;
"Chief and King of all the beavers."
But not long had Pau-Puk-Keewis
Sat in state among the beavers
When there came a voice of warning
From the watchman at his station
In the water-flags and lilies,
Saying, "Here is Hiawatha!
Hiawatha with his hunters!"
Then they heard a cry above them,
Heard a shouting and a tramping,
Heard a crashing and a rushing,
And the water round and o'er them
Sank and sucked away in eddies,
And they knew their dam was broken.
On the lodge's roof the hunters
Leaped, and broke it all asunder;
Streamed the sunshine through the crevice,
Sprang the beavers through the doorway,
Hid themselves in deeper water,
In the channel of the streamlet;
But the mighty Pau-Puk-Keewis
Could not pass beneath the doorway;
He was puffed with pride and feeding,
He was swollen like a bladder.
Through the roof looked Hiawatha,
Cried aloud, "O Pau-Puk-Keewis!
Vain are all your craft and cunning,
Vain your manifold disguises!
Well I know you, Pau-Puk-Keewis!"
With their clubs they beat and bruised him,
Beat to death poor Pau-Puk-Keewis
Pounded him as maize is pounded,
Till his skull was crushed to pieces.

Six tall hunters, lithe and limber,
Bore him home on poles and branches,
Bore the body of the beaver;
But the ghost, the Jeebi in him,
Thought and felt as Pau-Puk-Keewis,
Still lived on as Pau-Puk-Keewis.
And it fluttered, strove, and struggled,
Waving hither, waving thither,
As the curtains of a wigwam
Struggle with their thongs of deer-skin,
When the wintry wind is blowing;
Till it drew itself together,
Till it rose up from the body,
Till it took the form and features
Of the cunning Pau-Puk-Keewis
Vanishing into the forest.
But the wary Hiawatha
Saw the figure ere it vanished,
Saw the form of Pau-Puk-Keewis
Glide into the soft blue shadow
Of the pine-trees of the forest;
Toward the squares of white beyond it,
Toward an opening in the forest,
Like a wind it rushed and panted,
Bending all the boughs before it,
And behind it, as the rain comes,
Came the steps of Hiawatha.
To a lake with many islands
Came the breathless Pau-Puk-Keewis,
Where among the water-lilies
Pishnekuh, the brant, were sailing;
Through the tufts of rushes floating,
Steering through the reedy islands,
Now their broad black beaks they lifted,
Now they plunged beneath the water,
Now they darkened in the shadow,
Now they brightened in the sunshine.
"Pishnekuh!" cried Pau-Puk-Keewis,
"Pishnekuh! my brothers!" said he,
"Change me to a brant with plumage,
With a shining neck and feathers,
Make me large, and make me larger,
Ten times larger than the others."
Straightway to a brant they changed him,
With two huge and dusky pinions,
With a bosom smooth and rounded,
With a bill like two great paddles,
Made him larger than the others,
Ten times larger than the largest,
Just as, shouting from the forest,
On the shore stood Hiawatha.
Up they rose with cry and clamor,
With a whir and beat of pinions,
Rose up from the reedy islands,
From the water-flags and lilies.
And they said to Pau-Puk-Keewis:

"In your flying, look not downward,
Take good heed, and look not downward,
Lest some strange mischance should happen,
Lest some great mishap befall you!"
Fast and far they fled to northward,
Fast and far through mist and sunshine,
Fed among the moors and fen-lands,
Slept among the reeds and rushes.
On the morrow as they journeyed,
Buoyed and lifted by the South-wind,
Wafted onward by the South-wind,
Blowing fresh and strong behind them,
Rose a sound of human voices,
Rose a clamor from beneath them,
From the lodges of a village,
From the people miles beneath them.
For the people of the village
Saw the flock of brant with wonder,
Saw the wings of Pau-Puk-Keewis
Flapping far up in the ether,
Broader than two doorway curtains.
Pau-Puk-Keewis heard the shouting,
Knew the voice of Hiawatha,
Knew the outcry of Iagoo,
And, forgetful of the warning,
Drew his neck in, and looked downward,
And the wind that blew behind him
Caught his mighty fan of feathers,
Sent him wheeling, whirling downward.
All in vain did Pau-Puk-Keewis
Struggle to regain his balance;
Whirling round and round and downward,
He beheld in turn the village
And in turn the flock above him,
Saw the village coming nearer,
And the flock receding farther,
Heard the voices growing louder,
Heard the shouting and the laughter;
Saw no more the flock above him,
Only saw the earth beneath him;
Dead out of the empty heaven,
Dead among the shouting people,
With a heavy sound and sullen,
Fell the brant with broken pinions.
But his soul, his ghost, his shadow,
Still survived as Pau-Puk-Keewis,
Took again the form and features
Of the handsome Yenadizze,
And again went rushing onward,
Followed fast by Hiawatha,
Crying: "Not so wide the world is,
Not so long and rough the way is,
But my wrath shall overtake you,
But my vengeance shall attain you!"
And so near he came, so near him,
That his hand was stretched to seize him,

His right hand to seize and hold him,
When the cunning Pau-Puk-Keewis
Whirled and spun about in circles,
Fanned the air into a whirlwind,
Danced the dust and leaves about him,
And amid the whirling eddies
Sprang into a hollow oak-tree,
Changed himself into a serpent,
Gliding out through root and rubbish.
With his right hand Hiawatha
Smote amain the hollow oak-tree,
Rent it into shreds and splinters,
Left it lying there in fragments.
But in vain; for Pau-Puk-Keewis,
Once again in human figure,
Full in sight ran on before him,
Sped away in gust and whirlwind,
On the shores of Gitche Gumee,
Westward by the Big-Sea-Water,
Came unto the rocky headlands,
To the Pictured Rocks of sand-stone,
Looking over lake and landscape.
And the Old Man of the Mountain,
He the Manito of Mountains,
Opened wide his rocky doorways,
Opened wide his deep abysses,
Giving Pau-Puk-Keewis shelter
In his caverns dark and dreary,
Bidding Pau-Puk-Keewis welcome
To his gloomy lodge of sandstone.
There without stood Hiawatha,
Found the doorways closed against him,
With his mittens, Minjekahwun,
Smote great caverns in the sandstone,
Cried aloud in tones of thunder,
"Open! I am Hiawatha!"
But the Old Man of the Mountain
Opened not, and made no answer
From the silent crags of sandstone,
From the gloomy rock abysses.
Then he raised his hands to heaven,
Called imploring on the tempest,
Called Waywassimo, the lightning,
And the thunder, Annemeekee;
And they came with night and darkness
Sweeping down the Big-Sea-Water
From the distant Thunder Mountains;
And the trembling Pau-Puk-Keewis
Heard the footsteps of the thunder,
Saw the red eyes of the lightning,
Was afraid, and crouched and trembled.
Then Waywassimo, the lightning,
Smote the doorways of the caverns,
With his war-club smote the doorways,
Smote the jutting crags of sandstone,
And the thunder, Annemeekee,

Shouted down into the caverns,
Saying, "Where is Pau-Puk-Keewis!"
And the crags fell, and beneath them
Dead among the rocky ruins
Lay the cunning Pau-Puk-Keewis,
Lay the handsome Yenadizze,
Slain in his own human figure.
Ended were his wild adventures,
Ended were his tricks and gambols,
Ended all his craft and cunning,
Ended all his mischief-making,
All his gambling and his dancing,
All his wooing of the maidens.
Then the noble Hiawatha
Took his soul, his ghost, his shadow,
Spake and said: "O Pau-Puk-Keewis,
Never more in human figure
Shall you search for new adventures;
Never more with jest and laughter
Dance the dust and leaves in whirlwinds;
But above there in the heavens
You shall soar and sail in circles;
I will change you to an eagle,
To Keneu, the great war-eagle,
Chief of all the fowls with feathers,
Chief of Hiawatha's chickens."
And the name of Pau-Puk-Keewis
Lingers still among the people,
Lingers still among the singers,
And among the story-tellers;
And in Winter, when the snow-flakes
Whirl in eddies round the lodges,
When the wind in gusty tumult
O'er the smoke-flue pipes and whistles,
"There," they cry, "comes Pau-Puk-Keewis
He is dancing through the village,
He is gathering in his harvest!"

XVIII

THE DEATH OF KWASIND

FAR and wide among the nations
Spread the name and fame of Kwasind;
No man dared to strive with Kwasind,
No man could compete with Kwasind.
But the mischievous Puk-Wudjies,
They the envious Little People,
They the fairies and the pygmies,
Plotted and conspired against him.
"If the hateful Kwasind," said they,
"If this great, outrageous fellow
Goes on thus a little longer,
Tearing everything he touches,

Rending everything to pieces,
Filling all the world with wonder,
What becomes of the Puk-Wudjies!
Who will care for the Puk-Wudjies!
He will tread us down like mushrooms,
Drive us all into the water,
Give our bodies to be eaten
By the wicked Nee-ba-naw-baigs,
By the Spirits of the water!"
So the angry Little People
All conspired against the Strong Man,
All conspired to murder Kwasind,
Yes, to rid the world of Kwasind,
The audacious, overbearing,
Heartless, haughty, dangerous Kwasind!
Now this wondrous strength of Kwasind
In his crown alone was seated;
In his crown too was his weakness;
There alone could he be wounded,
Nowhere else could weapon pierce him,
Nowhere else could weapon harm him.
Even there the only weapon
That could wound him, that could slay him,
Was the seed-cone of the pine-tree,
Was the blue cone of the fir-tree.
This was Kwasind's fatal secret,
Known to no man among mortals;
But the cunning Little People,
The Puk-Wudjies, knew the secret,
Knew the only way to kill him.
So they gathered cones together,
Gathered seed-cones of the pine-tree,
Gathered blue cones of the fir-tree,
In the woods by Taquamenaw,
Brought them to the river's margin,
Heaped them in great piles together,
Where the red rocks from the margin
Jutting overhang the river.
There they lay in wait for Kwasind,
The malicious Little People.
'Twas an afternoon in Summer;
Very hot and still the air was,
Very smooth the gliding river,
Motionless the sleeping shadows;
Insects glistened in the sunshine,
Insects skated on the water,
Filled the drowsy air with buzzing,
With a far resounding war-cry.
Down the river came the Strong Man,
In his birch canoe came Kwasind,
Floating slowly down the current
Of the sluggish Taquamenaw,
Very languid with the weather,
Very sleepy with the silence.
From the overhanging branches,
From the tassels of the birch-trees,

Soft the Spirit of Sleep descended;
By his airy hosts surrounded,
His invisible attendants,
Came the Spirit of Sleep, Nepahwin;
Like the burnished Dush-kwo-ne-she,
Like a dragon-fly, he hovered
O'er the drowsy head of Kwasind.
To his ear there came a murmur
As of waves upon a sea-shore,
As of far-off tumbling waters,
As of winds among the pine-trees;
And he felt upon his forehead
Blows of little airy war-clubs,
Wielded by the slumbrous legions
Of the Spirit of Sleep, Nepahwin,
As of some one breathing on him.
At the first blow of their war-clubs,
Fell a drowsiness on Kwasind;
At the second blow they smote him,
Motionless his paddle rested;
At the third, before his vision

"HURLED THE PINE-CONES DOWN UPON HIM"—*Page 278*

Reeled the landscape into darkness,
Very sound asleep was Kwasind.
So he floated down the river,
Like a blind man seated upright,
Floated down the Taquamenaw.
Underneath the trembling birch-trees,
Underneath the wooded headlands.
Underneath the war encampment
Of the pygmies, the Puk-Wudjies.
There they stood, all armed and waiting,
Hurled the pine-cones down upon him,
Struck him on his brawny shoulders,
On his crown defenseless struck him.
"Death to Kwasind!" was the sudden
War-cry of the Little People.
And he sideways swayed and tumbled,
Sideways fell into the river,
Plunged beneath the sluggish water
Headlong, as an otter plunges;
And the birch-canoe, abandoned,
Drifted empty down the river,
Bottom upward swerved and drifted:
Nothing more was seen of Kwasind.
But the memory of the Strong Man
Lingered long among the people,
And whenever through the forest
Raged and roared the wintry tempest,
And the branches, tossed and troubled,
Creaked and groaned and split asunder,
"Kwasind!" cried they; "that is Kwasind!
He is gathering in his fire-wood!"

XIX

THE GHOSTS

NEVER stoops the soaring vulture
On his quarry in the desert,
On the sick or wounded bison,
But another vulture, watching
From his high aerial look-out,
Sees the downward plunge, and follows;
And a third pursues the second,
Coming from the invisible ether,
First a speck, and then a vulture,
Till the air is dark with pinions.
So disasters come not singly;
But as if they watched and waited,
Scanning one another's motions,
When the first descends, the others
Follow, follow, gather flock-wise
Round their victim, sick and wounded,
First a shadow, then a sorrow,
Till the air is dark with anguish.

Now, o'er all the dreary Northland,
Mighty Peboan, the Winter,
Breathing on the lakes and rivers,
Into stone had changed their waters.
From his hair he shook the snowflakes,
Till the plains were strewn with whiteness,
One uninterrupted level,
As if, stooping, the Creator
With his hands had smoothed them over.
Through the forest, wide and wailing,
Roamed the hunter on his snow-shoes;
In the village worked the women,
Pounded maize, or dressed the deer-skin;
And the young men played together
On the ice the noisy ball-play,
On the plain the dance of snow-shoes.
One dark evening, after sundown,
In her wigwam Laughing Water
Sat with old Nokomis, waiting
For the steps of Hiawatha
Homeward from the hunt returning.
On their faces gleamed the fire-light,
Painting them with streaks of crimson,
In the eyes of old Nokomis
Glimmered like the watery moonlight,
In the eyes of Laughing Water
Glistened like the sun in water;
And behind them crouched their shadows
In the corners of the wigwam,
And the smoke in wreaths above them
Climbed and crowded through the smoke-flue.
Then the curtain of the doorway
From without was slowly lifted;
Brighter glowed the fire a moment,
And a moment swerved the smoke-wreath,
As two women entered softly,
Passed the doorway uninvited,
Without word of salutation,
Without sign of recognition,
Sat down in the farthest corner,
Crouching low among the shadows.
From their aspect and their garments,
Strangers seemed they in the village;
Very pale and haggard were they,
As they sat there sad and silent,
Trembling, cowering with the shadows.
Was it the wind above the smoke-flue,
Muttering down into the wigwam?
Was it the owl, the Koko-koho,
Hooting from the dismal forest?
Sure a voice said in the silence:
"These are corpses clad in garments,
These are ghosts that come to haunt you,
From the kingdom of Ponemah,
From the land of the Hereafter!"
Homeward now came Hiawatha,

116

From his hunting in the forest,
With the snow upon his tresses,
And the red deer on his shoulders.
At the feet of Laughing Water
Down he threw his lifeless burden;
Nobler, handsomer she thought him
Than when he first came to woo her,
First threw down the deer before her,
As a token of his wishes,
As a promise of the future.
Then he turned and saw the strangers,
Cowering, crouching with the shadows,
Said within himself, "Who are they?
What strange guests hast Minnehaha?"
But he questioned not the strangers,
Only spake to bid them welcome
To his lodge, his food, his fireside.
When the evening meal was ready,
And the deer had been divided,
Both the pallid guests, the strangers,
Springing from among the shadows,
Seized upon the choicest portions,
Seized the white fat of the roebuck,
Set apart for Laughing Water,
For the wife of Hiawatha;
Without asking, without thanking,
Eagerly devoured the morsels,
Flitted back among the shadows
In the corner of the wigwam.
Not a word spake Hiawatha,
Not a motion made Nokomis,
Not a gesture Laughing Water;
Not a change came o'er their features,
Only Minnehaha softly
Whispered, saying, "They are famished;
Let them do what best delights them;
Let them eat, for they are famished."
Many a daylight dawned and darkened,
Many a night shook off the daylight
As the pine shakes off the snow-flakes
From the midnight of its branches;
Day by day the guests unmoving
Sat there silent in the wigwam;
But by night, in storm or starlight,
Forth they went into the forest,
Bringing fire-wood to the wigwam,
Bringing pine-cones for the burning,
Always sad and always silent.
And whenever Hiawatha
Came from fishing or from hunting,
When the evening meal was ready,
And the food had been divided,
Gliding from their darksome corner,
Came the pallid guests, the strangers,
Seized upon the choicest portions
Set aside for Laughing Water,

And without rebuke or question
Flitted back among the shadows.
Never once had Hiawatha
By a word or look reproved them;
Never once had old Nokomis
Made a gesture of impatience;
Never once had Laughing Water
Shown resentment at the outrage.
All had they endured in silence,
That the rights of guest and stranger,
That the virtue of free-giving,
By a look might not be lessened,
By a word might not be broken.
Once at midnight Hiawatha,
Ever wakeful, ever watchful,
In the wigwam, dimly lighted
By the brands that still were burning,
By the glimmering, flickering firelight,
Heard a sighing, oft repeated,
Heard a sobbing, as of sorrow.
From his couch rose Hiawatha,
From his shaggy hides of bison,
Pushed aside the deer-skin curtain,
Saw the pallid guests, the shadows,
Sitting upright on their couches,
Weeping in the silent midnight.
And he said: "O guests! why is it
That your hearts are so afflicted,
That you sob so in the midnight?
Has perchance the old Nokomis,
Has my wife, my Minnehaha,
Wronged or grieved you by unkindness,
Failed in hospitable duties?"
Then the shadows ceased from weeping,
Ceased from sobbing and lamenting,
And they said, with gentle voices
"We are ghosts of the departed,
Souls of those who once were with you.
From the realms of Chibiabos
Hither have we come to try you,
Hither have we come to warn you.
"Cries of grief and lamentation
Reach us in the Blessed Islands;
Cries of anguish from the living,
Calling back their friends departed,
Sadden us with useless sorrow.
Therefore have we come to try you;
No one knows us, no one heeds us.
We are but a burden to you,
And we see that the departed
Have no place among the living.
"Think of this, O Hiawatha!
Speak of it to all the people,
That henceforward and forever
They no more with lamentations
Sadden the souls of the departed

In the Islands of the Blessed.
"Do not lay such heavy burdens
In the graves of those you bury,
Not such weight of furs and wampum,
Not such weight of pots and kettles,
For the spirits faint beneath them.
Only give them food to carry,
Only give them fire to light them.
"Four days is the spirit's journey
To the land of ghosts and shadows,
Four its lonely night encampments;
Four times must their fires be lighted.
Therefore, when the dead are buried,
Let a fire, as night approaches,
Four times on the grave be kindled,
That the soul upon its journey
May not lack the cheerful fire-light,
May not grope about in darkness.
"Farewell, noble Hiawatha!
We have put you to the trial,
To the proof have put your patience,
By the insult of our presence,
By the outrage of our actions.
We have found you great and noble.
Fail not in the greater trial,
Faint not in the harder struggle."
When they ceased, a sudden darkness
Fell and filled the silent wigwam.
Hiawatha heard a rustle
As of garments trailing by him,
Heard the curtain of the doorway
Lifted by a hand he saw not,
Felt the cold breath of the night air,
For a moment saw the starlight;
But he saw the ghosts no longer,
Saw no more the wandering spirits
From the kingdom of Ponemah,
From the land of the Hereafter.

XX

THE FAMINE

O THE long and dreary Winter!
O the cold and cruel Winter!
Ever thicker, thicker, thicker
Froze the ice on lake and river,
Ever deeper, deeper, deeper
Fell the snow o'er all the landscape,
Fell the covering snow, and drifted
Through the forest, round the village.
Hardly from his buried wigwam
Could the hunter force a passage;
With his mittens and his snow-shoes

119

Vainly walked he through the forest,
Sought for bird or beast and found none,
Saw no track of deer or rabbit,
In the snow beheld no footprints,
In the ghastly, gleaming forest
Fell, and could not rise from weakness,
Perished there from cold and hunger.
O the famine and the fever!
O the wasting of the famine!
O the blasting of the fever!
O the wailing of the children!
O the anguish of the women!
All the earth was sick and famished;
Hungry was the air around them,
Hungry was the sky above them,
And the hungry stars in heaven
Like the eyes of wolves glared at them!
Into Hiawatha's wigwam
Came two other guests, as silent
As the ghosts were, and as gloomy,
Waited not to be invited,
Did not parley at the doorway,
Sat there without word of welcome
In the seat of Laughing Water;
Looked with haggard eyes and hollow
At the face of Laughing Water.
And the foremost said: "Behold me!
I am Famine, Bukadawin!"
And the other said: "Behold me!
I am Fever, Ahkosewin!"
And the lovely Minnehaha
Shuddered as they looked upon her,
Shuddered at the words they uttered,
Lay down on her bed in silence,
Hid her face, but made no answer;
Lay there trembling, freezing, burning
At the looks they cast upon her,
At the fearful words they uttered.
Forth into the empty forest
Rushed the maddened Hiawatha;
In his heart was deadly sorrow,
In his face a stony firmness;
On his brow the sweat of anguish
Started, but it froze and fell not.
Wrapped in furs and armed for hunting,
With his mighty bow of ash-tree,
With his quiver full of arrows,
With his mittens, Minjekahwun,
Into the vast and vacant forest
On his snow-shoes strode he forward.
"Gitche Manito, the Mighty!"
Cried he with his face uplifted
In that bitter hour of anguish,
"Give your children food, O Father!
Give us food, or we must perish!
Give me food for Minnehaha,

For my dying Minnehaha!"
Through the far-resounding forest,
Through the forest vast and vacant
Rang that cry of desolation,
But there came no other answer
Than the echo of his crying,
Than the echo of the woodlands,
"Minnehaha! Minnehaha!"
All day long roved Hiawatha
In that melancholy forest,
Through the shadow of whose thickets,
In the pleasant days of Summer,
Of that ne'er forgotten Summer,
He had brought his young wife homeward
From the land of the Dacotahs;
When the birds sang in the thickets,
And the streamlets laughed and glistened,
And the air was full of fragrance,
And the lovely Laughing Water
Said, with voice that did not tremble:
"I will follow you, my husband!"
In the wigwam with Nokomis
With those gloomy guests, that watched her,
With the Famine and the Fever,
She was lying, the Beloved,
She the dying Minnehaha.
"Hark!" she said; "I hear a rushing,
Hear a roaring and a rushing,
Hear the Falls of Minnehaha
Calling to me from a distance!"
"No, my child!" said old Nokomis,
"'Tis the night-wind in the pine-trees!"
"Look!" she said; "I see my father
Standing lonely at his doorway,
Beckoning to me from his wigwam
In the land of the Dacotahs!"
"No, my child!" said old Nokomis,
"'Tis the smoke, that waves and beckons!"
"Ah!" said she, "the eyes of Pauguk
Glare upon me in the darkness,
I can feel his icy fingers
Clasping mine amid the darkness!
Hiawatha! Hiawatha!"
And the desolate Hiawatha,
Far away amid the forest,
Miles away among the mountains,
Heard that sudden cry of anguish,
Heard the voice of Minnehaha
Calling to him in the darkness,
"Hiawatha! Hiawatha!"
Over the snow-fields waste and pathless,
Under snow-encumbered branches,
Homeward hurried Hiawatha,
Empty-handed, heavy-hearted,
Heard Nokomis moaning, wailing:
"Wahonowin! Wahonowin!

Would that I had perished for you,
Would that I were dead as you are!
Wahonowin! Wahonowin!"
And he rushed into the wigwam,
Saw the old Nokomis slowly
Rocking to and fro and moaning,
Saw his lovely Minnehaha
Lying dead and cold before him,
And his bursting heart within him
Uttered such a cry of anguish
That the forest moaned and shuddered,
That the very stars in heaven
Shook and trembled with his anguish.
Then he sat down, still and speechless,
On the bed of Minnehaha,
At the feet of Laughing Water,
At those willing feet, that never
More would lightly run to meet him,
Never more would lightly follow.
With both hands his face he covered,
Seven long days and nights he sat there,
As if in a swoon he sat there,
Speechless, motionless, unconscious
Of the daylight or the darkness.
Then he buried Minnehaha;
In the snow a grave they made her,
In the forest deep and darksome,
Underneath the moaning hemlocks;
Clothed her in her richest garments,
Wrapped her in her robes of ermine;
Covered her with snow, like ermine,
Thus they buried Minnehaha.
And at night a fire was lighted,
On her grave four times was kindled,
For her soul upon its journey
To the Islands of the Blessed.
From his doorway Hiawatha
Saw it burning in the forest,
Lighting up the gloomy hemlocks;
From his sleepless bed uprising,
From the bed of Minnehaha,
Stood and watched it at the doorway,
That it might not be extinguished,
Might not leave her in the darkness.
"Farewell!" said he, "Minnehaha!
Farewell, O my Laughing Water!
All my heart is buried with you,
All my thoughts go onward with you!
Come not back again to labor,
Come not back again to suffer,
Where the Famine and the Fever
Wear the heart and waste the body.
Soon my task will be completed,
Soon your footsteps I shall follow
To the Islands of the Blessed,
To the Kingdom of Ponemah,

XXI

THE WHITE MAN'S FOOT

IN his lodge beside a river,
Close beside a frozen river,
Sat an old man, sad and lonely.
White his hair was as a snow-drift;
Dull and low his fire was burning,
And the old man shook and trembled,
Folded in his Waubewyon,
In his tattered white skin-wrapper,
Hearing nothing but the tempest
As it roared along the forest,
Seeing nothing but the snow-storm,
As it whirled and hissed and drifted.
All the coals were white with ashes,
And the fire was slowly dying,
As a young man, walking lightly,
At the open doorway entered.
Red with blood of youth his cheeks were,
Soft his eyes, as stars in Spring-time,
Bound his forehead was with grasses,
Bound and plumed with scented grasses;
On his lips a smile of beauty,
Filling all the lodge with sunshine,
In his hand a bunch of blossoms
Filling all the lodge with sweetness.
"Ah, my son!" exclaimed the old man,
"Happy are my eyes to see you.
Sit here on the mat beside me,
Sit here by the dying embers;
Let us pass the night together.
Tell me of your strange adventures,
Of the lands where you have travelled;
I will tell you of my prowess,
Of my many deeds of wonder."
From his pouch he drew his peace-pipe,
Very old and strangely fashioned,
Made of red stone was the pipe-head,
And the stem a reed with feathers,
Filled the pipe with bark of willow,
Placed a burning coal upon it,
Gave it to his guest, the stranger;
And began to speak in this wise:
"When I blow my breath about me,
When I breathe upon the landscape,
Motionless are all the rivers,
Hard as stone becomes the water!"
And the young man answered, smiling:
"When I blow my breath about me,
When I breathe upon the landscape,

Flowers spring up o'er all the meadows,
Singing, onward rush the rivers!"
"When I shake my hoary tresses,"
Said the old man, darkly frowning,
"All the land with snow is covered;
All the leaves from all the branches
Fall and fade and die and wither,
For I breathe, and lo! they are not.
From the waters and the marshes
Rise the wild goose and the heron,
Fly away to distant regions,
For I speak, and lo! they are not.
And where'er my footsteps wander,
All the wild beasts of the forest
Hide themselves in holes and caverns,
And the earth becomes as flint-stone!"
"When I shake my flowing ringlets,"
Said the young man, softly laughing,
"Showers of rain fall warm and welcome,
Plants lift up their heads rejoicing,
Back unto their lakes and marshes
Come the wild goose and the heron,
Homeward shoots the arrowy swallow,
Sing the bluebird and the robin,
And where'er my footsteps wander,
All the meadows wave with blossoms,
All the woodlands ring with music,
All the trees are dark with foliage!"
While they spake, the night departed;
From the distant realms of Wabun,
From his shining lodge of silver,
Like a warrior robed and painted,
Came the sun, and said, "Behold me!
Gheezis, the great sun, behold me!"
Then the old man's tongue was speechless.
And the air grew warm and pleasant,
And upon the wigwam sweetly
Sang the bluebird and the robin,
And the stream began to murmur,
And a scent of growing grasses
Through the lodge was gently wafted.
And Segwun, the youthful stranger,
More distinctly in the daylight
Saw the icy face before him:
It was Peboan, the Winter!
From his eyes the tears were flowing,
As from melting lakes the streamlets,
And his body shrank and dwindled
As the shouting sun ascended,
Till into the air it faded,
Till into the ground it vanished,
And the young man saw before him,
On the hearth-stone of the wigwam,
Where the fire had smoked and smouldered,
Saw the earliest flower of Spring-time
Saw the beauty of the Spring-time.

Saw the Miskodeed in blossom.
Thus it was that in the North-land
After that unheard-of coldness,
That intolerable Winter,
Came the Spring with all its splendor.
All its birds and all its blossoms,
All its flowers and leaves and grasses.
Sailing on the wind to northward,
Flying in great flocks, like arrows,
Like huge arrows shot through heaven,
Passed the swan, the Mahnahbezee,
Speaking almost as a man speaks;
And in long lines waving, bending
Like a bow-string snapped asunder,
Came the white goose, Waw-be-wawa:
And the pairs or singly flying,
Mahng the loon, with clangorous pinions,
The blue heron, the Shuh-shuh-gah,
And the grouse, the Mushkodasa.
In the thickets, and the meadows
Piped the bluebird, the Owaissa,
On the summit of the lodges
Sang the Opechee, the robin,
In the cover of the pine-trees
Cooed the pigeon, the Omemee,
And the sorrowing Hiawatha,
Speechless in his infinite sorrow,
Heard their voices calling to him,
Went forth from his gloomy doorway,
Stood and gazed into the heaven,
Gazed upon the earth and waters.
From his wanderings far to eastward,
From the regions of the morning,
From the shining land of Wabun,
Homeward now returned Iagoo,
The great traveller, the great boaster,
Full of new and strange adventures,
Marvels many and many wonders.
And the people of the village
Listened to him as he told them
Of his marvellous adventures,
Laughing answered him in this wise:
"Ugh! it is indeed Iagoo!
No one else beholds such wonders!"
He had seen, he said, a water
Bigger than the Big-Sea-Water,
Broader than the Gitche Gumee,
Bitter so that none could drink it!
At each other looked the warriors,
Looked the women at each other,
Smiled and said, "It cannot be so!
Kaw!" they said, "It cannot be so!"
O'er it, said he, o'er this water
Came a great canoe with pinions,
A canoe with wings came flying,
Bigger than a grove of pine-trees,

Taller than the tallest tree-tops!"
And the old men and the women
Looked and tittered at each other;
"Kaw!" they said, "we don't believe it!"
From its mouth, he said, to greet him,
Came Waywassimo, the lightning,
Came the thunder, Annemeekee!
And the warriors and the women
Laughed aloud at poor Iagoo;
"Kaw!" they said, "what tales you tell us!"
In it, said he, came a people,
In the great canoe with pinions
Came, he said, a hundred warriors;
Painted white were all their faces
And with hair their chins were covered!"
And the warriors and the women
Laughed and shouted in derision,
Like the ravens on the tree-tops,
Like the crows upon the hemlocks.
"Kaw!" they said, "what lies you tell us!
Do not think that we believe them!"
Only Hiawatha laughed not,
But he gravely spake and answered
To their jeering and their jesting:
"True is all Iagoo tells us;
I have seen it in a vision,
Seen the great canoe with pinions,
Seen the people with white faces,
Seen the coming of this bearded
People of the wooden vessel
From the regions of the morning,
From the shining land of Wabun.
"Gitche Manito, the Mighty,
The Great Spirit, the Creator,
Sends them hither on his errand,
Sends them to us with his message.
Wheresoe'er they move, before them
Swarms the stinging fly, the Ahmo,
Swarms the bee, the honey-maker;
Wheresoe'er they tread, beneath them
Springs a flower unknown among us,
Springs the White-man's Foot in blossom.
"Let us welcome, then, the strangers,
Hail them as our friends and brothers,
And the heart's right hand of friendship
Give them when they come to see us.
Gitche Manito, the Mighty,
Said this to me in my vision.
"I beheld, too, in that vision
All the secrets of the future,
Of the distant days that shall be.
I beheld the westward marches
Of the unknown, crowded nations.
All the land was full of people,
Restless, struggling, toiling, striving,
Speaking many tongues, yet feeling

But one heart-beat in their bosoms.
In the woodlands rang their axes,
Smoked their towns in all the valleys,
Over all the lakes and rivers
Rushed their great canoes of thunder.
"Then a darker, drearier vision
Passed before me, vague and cloudlike
I beheld our nation scattered,
All forgetful of my counsels,
Weakened, warring with each other;
Saw the remnants of our people
Sweeping westward, wild and woeful,
Like the cloud-rack of a tempest,
Like the withered leaves of Autumn!"

XXII

HIAWATHA'S DEPARTURE

BY the shore of Gitche Gumee,
By the shining Big-Sea-Water,
At the doorway of his wigwam,
In the pleasant Summer morning,
Hiawatha stood and waited.
All the air was full of freshness,
All the earth was bright and joyous,
And before him, through the sunshine,
Westward toward the neighboring forest
Passed in golden swarms the Ahmo,
Passed the bees, the honey-makers,
Burning, singing in the sunshine.
Bright above him shone the heavens,
Level spread the lake before him;
From its bosom leaped the sturgeon,
Sparkling, flashing in the sunshine;
On its margin the great forest
Stood reflected in the water,
Every tree-top had its shadow,
Motionless beneath the water.
From the brow of Hiawatha
Gone was every trace of sorrow,
As the fog from off the water,
As the mist from off the meadow.
With a smile of joy and triumph,
With a look of exultation,
As of one who in a vision
Sees what is to be, but is not,
Stood and waited Hiawatha.
Toward the sun his hands were lifted,
Both the palms spread out against it,
And between the parted fingers
Fell the sunshine on his features,
Flecked with light his naked shoulders,
As it falls and flecks an oak-tree

Through the rifted leaves and branches.
O'er the water floating, flying,
Something in the hazy distance,
Something in the mists of morning,
Loomed and lifted from the water,
Now seemed floating, now seemed flying,
Coming nearer, nearer, nearer.
Was it Shingebis, the diver?
Was it the pelican, the Shada?
Or the heron, the Shuh-shuh-gah?
Or the white goose, Waw-be-wawa,
With the water dripping, flashing,
From its glossy neck and feathers?
It was neither goose nor diver,
Neither pelican nor heron,
O'er the water floating, flying,
Through the shining mist of morning,
But a birch-canoe with paddles,
Rising, sinking on the water,
Dripping, flashing in the sunshine;
And within it came a people
From the distant land of Wabun,
From the farthest realms of morning
Came the Black-Robe chief, the Prophet,
He the Priest of Prayer, the Pale-face,
With his guides and his companions.
And the noble Hiawatha,
With his hands aloft extended,
Held aloft in sign of welcome,
Waited, full of exultation,
Till the birch-canoe with paddles
Grated on the shining pebbles,
Stranded on the sandy margin,
Till the Black-Robe chief, the Pale-face,
With the cross upon his bosom,
Landed on the sandy margin.
Then the joyous Hiawatha
Cried aloud and spake in this wise:
"Beautiful is the sun, O strangers,
When you come so far to see us!
All our town in peace awaits you,
All our doors stand open for you;
You shall enter all our wigwams,
For the heart's right hand we give you.
"Never bloomed the earth so gayly,
Never shone the sun so brightly,
As to-day they shine and blossom,
When you come so far to see us!
Never was our lake so tranquil,
Nor so free from rocks and sand-bars;
For your birch-canoe in passing
Has removed both rock and sand-bar.
"Never before had our tobacco
Such a sweet and pleasant flavor,
Never the broad leaves of our cornfields
Were so beautiful to look on

As they seem to us this morning,
When you come so far to see us!"
And the Black-Robe chief made answer,
Stammered in his speech a little,
Speaking words yet unfamiliar:
"Peace be with you, Hiawatha,
Peace be with you and your people,
Peace of prayer, and peace of pardon,
Peace of Christ, and joy of Mary!"
Then the generous Hiawatha
Led the strangers to his wigwam,
Seated them on skins of bison,
Seated them on skins of ermine,
And the careful old Nokomis
Brought them food in bowls of bass-wood,
Water brought in birchen dippers,
And the calumet, the peace-pipe,
Filled and lighted for their smoking.
All the old men of the village,
All the warriors of the nation,
All the Jossakeeds, the prophets,
The magicians, the Wabenos,
And the medicine-men, the Medas,
Came to bid the strangers welcome:
"It is well," they said, "O brothers,
That you come so far to see us!"
In a circle round the doorway,
With their pipes they sat in silence,
Waiting to behold the strangers,
Waiting to receive their message;
Till the Black-Robe chief, the Pale-face,
From the wigwam came to greet them,
Stammering in his speech a little,
Speaking words yet unfamiliar;
"It is well," they said, "O brother,
When you come so far to see us!"
Then the Black-Robe chief, the prophet,
Told his message to the people,
Told the purport of his mission,
Told them of the Virgin Mary,
And her blessed Son, the Saviour,
How in distant lands and ages
He had lived on earth as we do;
How he fasted, prayed, and labored;
How the Jews, the tribe accursed,
Mocked him, scourged him, crucified him;
How he rose from where they laid him,
Walked again with his disciples,
And ascended into heaven.
And the chiefs made answer saying:
"We have listened to your message,
We have heard your words of wisdom,
We will think on what you tell us.
It is well for us, O brothers,
That you come so far to see us!"

"WESTWARD, WESTWARD, HIAWATHA
SAILED INTO THE FIERY SUNSET"—*Page 312*

Then they rose up and departed
Each one homeward to his wigwam,
To the young men and the women
Told the story of the strangers
Whom the Master of Life had sent them
From the shining land of Wabun.
Heavy with the heat and silence
Grew the afternoon of Summer;
With a drowsy sound the forest
Whispered round the sultry wigwam,
With a sound of sleep the water
Rippled on the beach below it;
From the cornfields shrill and ceaseless
Sang the grasshopper, Pah-puk-keena;
And the guests of Hiawatha,
Weary with the heat of Summer,
Slumbered in the sultry wigwam.
Slowly o'er the simmering landscape
Fell the evening's dusk and coolness,
And the long and level sunbeams
Shot their spears into the forest,
Breaking through its shields of shadow,

130

Rushed into each secret ambush,
Searched each thicket, dingle, hollow;
Still the guests of Hiawatha
Slumbered in the silent wigwam.
From his place rose Hiawatha,
Bade farewell to old Nokomis,
Spake in whispers, spake in this wise,
Did not wake the guests, that slumbered:
"I am going, O Nokomis,
On a long and distant journey,
To the portals of the Sunset,
To the regions of the Home-wind,
Of the Northwest wind, Keewaydin.
But these guests I leave behind me,
In your watch and ward I leave them;
See that never harm comes near them,
See that never fear molests them,
Never danger nor suspicion,
Never want of food or shelter,
In the lodge of Hiawatha!"
Forth into the village went he,
Bade farewell to all the warriors,
Bade farewell to all the young men,
Spake persuading, spake in this wise:
"I am going, O my people,
On a long and distant journey;
Many moons and many winters
Will have come and will have vanished.
Ere I come again to see you.
But my guests I leave behind me;
Listen to their words of wisdom,
Listen to the truth they tell you,
For the Master of Life has sent them
From the land of light and morning!"
On the shore stood Hiawatha,
Turned and waved his hand at parting;
On the clear and luminous water
Launched his birch-canoe for sailing,
From the pebbles of the margin
Shoved it forth into the water;
Whispered to it, "Westward! westward!"
And with speed it darted forward.
And the evening sun descending
Set the clouds on fire with redness,
Burned the broad sky, like a prairie,
Left upon the level water
One long track and trail of splendor,
Down whose stream, as down a river,
Westward, westward Hiawatha
Sailed into the fiery sunset,
Sailed into the purple vapors,
Sailed into the dusk of evening.
And the people from the margin
Watched him floating, rising, sinking,
Till the birch canoe seemed lifted
High into that sea of splendor,

Till it sank into the vapors
Like the new moon slowly, slowly
Sinking in the purple distance.
And they said, "Farewell forever!"
Said, "Farewell, O Hiawatha!"
And the forests, dark and lonely,
Moved through all their depths of darkness,
Sighed, "Farewell, O Hiawatha!"
And the waves upon the margin
Rising, rippling on the pebbles,
Sobbed, "Farewell, O Hiawatha!"
And the heron, the Shuh-shuh-gah,
From her haunts among the fen-lands
Screamed, "Farewell, O Hiawatha!"
Thus departed Hiawatha,
Hiawatha, the Beloved,
In the glory of the sunset,
In the purple mists of evening,
To the regions of the home-wind,
Of the Northwest wind Keewaydin,
To the Islands of the Blessed,
To the kingdom of Ponemah,
To the land of the Hereafter!

THE END

9 781518 737404